# PRAISE FOR TOM MOORE

## Angels Crying

"This is a truly compelling book . . . carefully researched, well documented and sensitively written . . . highlights the failure of protective services, police and child welfare to protect children. The writer's skill is such that this book reads like a novel. . . . It should be required reading for foster parents, social workers, police and for students in the helping professions."

INTERNATIONAL JOURNAL OF FAMILY CARE

"The book gathers steam like a locomotive, reaching a fevered, page-turning pitch. *Angels Crying* is a good read."

THE SUNDAY EXPRESS

"It's a well written, well researched and well developed story. It will make you think. *Angels Crying* is a gripping, heart-rending story you'll have a tough time putting down."

THE NEWFOUNDLAND HERALD

"I hope *Angels Crying* will be widely read . . . solidly readable, heartbreaking book . . . an excellent job . . ."

THE TELEGRAM

# PRAISE FOR TOM MOORE

## Good-bye Momma

"*Good-bye Momma* by Tom Moore is a genuinely touching novel about a little boy . . . who must cope with the pain of his mother's early death and his father's remarriage."

CHATELAINE MAGAZINE

"This writer puts more in 70 pages than most authors can put in 300. The story is so full of incident, of character, of feeling . . ."

IN REVIEW

"Most of all he is a strongly believable juvenile character with a background that will be exotic for children his age and older . . ."

THE TORONTO STAR

"Tom Moore has written a story of childhood in Newfoundland outports, a tale vividly told in a style as fresh as a coastal breeze, and presenting the fears, passions and glories of young children in a very sympathetic way."

PERCY JANES

"Great art is always the emergence of the universal from the particular . . . Tom Moore's novel, *Good-bye Momma*, is an excellent example of writers throughout the country who wear the badge of the particular proudly."

EMERGENCY LIBRARIAN

# THE SIGN

## ~ ON MY ~

# FATHER'S

# HOUSE

*Tom Moore*

# THE SIGN

## ~ ON MY ~

## FATHER'S

# HOUSE

## TOM MOORE

FLANKER PRESS LIMITED
ST. JOHN'S

**Library and Archives Canada Cataloguing in Publication**

Title: The sign on my father's house : a novel / Tom Moore.
Names: Moore, Tom, 1950- author.
Identifiers: Canadiana (print) 20190064668 | Canadiana (ebook) 20190064706 | ISBN 9781771177412 (softcover) | ISBN 9781771177429 (EPUB) | ISBN 9781771177436 (Kindle) | ISBN 9781771177443 (PDF)
Classification: LCC PS8576.O616 S54 2019 | DDC C813/.54—dc23

**PRINTED IN CANADA**

MIX
Paper from responsible sources
FSC® C016245

This paper has been certified to meet the environmental and social standards of the Forest Stewardship Council® (FSC®) and comes from responsibly managed forests, and verified recycled sources.

Cover design by Graham Blair

FLANKER PRESS LTD.
PO BOX 2522, STATION C
ST. JOHN'S, NL
CANADA

TELEPHONE: (709) 739-4477 FAX: (709) 739-4420 TOLL-FREE: 1-866-739-4420
WWW.FLANKERPRESS.COM

9 8 7 6 5 4 3 2 1

Canada

Canada Council for the Arts    Conseil des Arts du Canada

Newfoundland Labrador

We acknowledge the [financial] support of the Government of Canada. *Nous reconnaissons l'appui [financier] du gouvernement du Canada.* We acknowledge the support of the Canada Council for the Arts, which last year invested $153 million to bring the arts to Canadians throughout the country. *Nous remercions le Conseil des arts du Canada de son soutien. L'an dernier, le Conseil a investi 153 millions de dollars pour mettre de l'art dans la vie des Canadiennes et des Canadiens de tout le pays.* We acknowledge the financial support of the Government of Newfoundland and Labrador, Department of Tourism, Culture and Recreation for our publishing activities.

# CONTENTS

For Gerald Squires (1937–2016)

# INTRODUCTION

This is the story of a young man finding his way through life. It is set in Newfoundland at the end of the Smallwood era, when we looked about for our identity as a people. We were now Canadians. What did that mean? It is a story about a father and a son and their constant love through conflicts and troubled times.

# 1

## Spring

Ah, love! On a bright May morning in 1966, I fell in love with Ellen Monteau. I was thirteen, and she was a senior student at Smallwood High. I had been invited to the senior classroom to report on a book I had read, *Gone with the Wind*. Sitting in the front row was the most beautiful human being I had ever seen.

Other students slouched in their desks, ignored me, or did homework. Someone hissed, "Shut up, Rhett Butler!" But when I finished my book report, distinct applause came from her desk. The bell rang, and twenty students barrelled past me out the door.

"The title tells it all, *Gone with the Wind*," she said breezily. She wafted toward me, and the warm sunlight followed her, trapped in her blonde hair. To me she looked about eight feet tall. She wore a pleated plaid skirt and a white cotton blouse with frills across the breast.

"Thank you," I croaked.

"It is truly divine . . ." Five minutes of bliss followed as the voice, which had acquired a slight southern accent, discussed the book. Atlanta burned, a civilization died before me, but I heard only her sweet voice, perhaps from Tara.

Behind me, several light years away, I heard another voice: "That was a fine job, Felix. You must have enjoyed the book very much," said the teacher. When I turned back, my vision from Dixie had disappeared into the Atlanta smoke. Sigh!

Out in the bumpy, tussling corridor of student bodies, Tammy Fagan was the first familiar face. "Who's the movie star in 11-A?" I asked.

Tammy shifted her books to her skinny hip and her gum to the other side of her mouth. "That would be Ellen Monteau. Aroused, are we, Felix? Ha ha! You'll be studying wet dreams in Family Living next year." She snorted, clutched her books to her skinny chest, and went on her way.

*Who is Ellen Monteau?* I needed to speak to Monk.

Outside the library door, Victoria Spaulding was standing on a chair, stapling a sign to the wall. She was on tiptoes, reaching high over her head, and hammering a staple gun with her fist.

I pretended not to notice her pleated skirt riding high over the backs of her legs.

"Just a minute, Felix."

I slunk by.

"Felix! Come here." She was the student president and head cheerleader of Smallwood High.

She looked down at me. "What grade are you in?"

"Nine," I said.

"Your class is allowed to attend the basketball game Friday night."

"But that goes on till late."

"I know. Mr. Banion will be contacting parents to let them know you're allowed. Isn't that wonderful? It was the student council's idea." She turned back to her sign.

I found Monk in the library. "The council needs the money," he said. "Two bucks a head, times sixty grade nines, makes a hundred and twenty bucks. Letting in your class puts them back in the black."

Monk's real name was Jerome Banion. We called him Monk because he spent every free minute alone in the library, like an old monk transcribing Greek into Latin. He was grossly overweight and sat atop his library chair like a frog on a mushroom. Monk remembered everything he read or heard. He'd moved to Curlew from some private school in Ontario, and I often wondered why his father had taken his family to Newfoundland. Where was Mrs. Banion? And I bet a divorce court was involved. Kids didn't like Monk, and no one spoke to him unless they had to. But I felt some small kinship because my father was a mainlander, too, from Alberta.

Monk knew everything. He could recite verbatim telephone conversations between his father and the school superintendent.

"I need to talk to you about something else," I said. His watery eyes moved up from the book in front of him. His chins jiggled as he shifted to a more comfortable position on his mushroom.

"Who is Ellen Monteau?"

"Well-developed blonde, room 11-A. Straight-A student. Lives with her mother in Petley. My kind of girl!" he concluded with a smile. His big head was already lowering back to his book.

"Sure is pretty," I said.

"Somewhat of a checkered past, though."

"What do you mean?"

Information was Monk's currency. With it he bought what little interaction he had with other human beings. "Something about her mother."

"What?"

Monk looked at me, then around the room. He pulled his chair closer to mine. "Okay, I'll tell you. The mother went to St. John's as a secretary years ago and came home pregnant. That was Ellen. They lived with the grandmother until the old lady died a few years ago. She must have left them the trailer. The mother drinks a lot, and there are men."

"Men?"

"Yeah, men. You'll do it next year in Family Living."

"I know, along with wet dreams."

"You're a bit young to be talking like that, aren't you?"

I walked home that evening with my next-door neighbour, Jeffery Williams. Jeff was a foot taller than me, and was the school basketball star. His hair was dark, fine, but already thinning. His body reminded me of a deer. He walked with his books bound with a leather belt and balanced on his head. Suddenly, he whirled around and lobbed five pounds of books up into an imaginary basket and caught them, shouting, "Two points! Going to the big game next Friday, Felix?"

"I don't know."

"Argentia Killers and us. Who do you think'll win?"

"I don't know."

"Shit, Felix! No one knows. Who do you *think* will win?"

"You, I guess."

"You bet! By eight points! Wait and see! I'll score thirty!"

I turned to go into my yard. "See you, Jeff." He just waved.

I entered the backyard. In the afternoon sun, two spring robins chirped in our apple tree. I went in the back door, threw my books on the woodbox, and hung up my coat in the porch.

Shirley, my stepmom, was at the kitchen table, and I could see she'd been crying. Her big dark eyes were ringed with red. She took a long sip of her tea and looked at me over the cup.

"Oh, Felix." More tears threatened, but she swallowed them with her tea. "He's at it again. He's out in the stable now. Go out and try to stop him." She looked out the window.

In the stable, I found my father hammering away in grim determination. "Felix, how are you, boy? Back from school. Good. You can help me with this thing." He wore a little paper painter's cap with a black shiny bib. Even in warm weather he wore a plaid shirt. He never wore jeans, but old pants for working and his new ones for church. He wasn't a tall man, but he was wide across the shoulders and thick through the chest. His receding hair was dark and curly and peeped out from under the paper cap. He was forty-three years old.

Father had before him a huge sign onto which he was hammering a frame. Upside down, it read something like DOG MAD WOOD SMALL, which made no sense to me.

I immediately began to help him.

The sign was impressive. He had painted the eight-foot-by-four-foot plywood sheet with white oil paint. Onto this went his large red letters. He finished hammering the fine blue frame and righted it for me to see, looking very pleased with his creation.

Now the words made some sense: GOD DAM SMALL-WOOD! It was a reference to the most popular man in Newfoundland: premier, governor, king, Joseph R. Smallwood. I preferred my first reading about the mad dog in the small wood.

"Isn't it a beauty, Felix? This will stir them up." He smiled, and a drop of spittle glistened on his chin. He wiped his hand across the slick sign to make sure the paint was dry. "All we need to do now is nail it to the house."

"Front or back?" I feared the worst.

"Felix! Felix! If we nail it to the back, no one will see it, boy. We need people to see it and read it for our ideas to strike home."

Here was a logic that could not be denied, so we nailed the sign to the front of our house.

My father wobbled on the top of the old wooden ladder. I held the rungs to keep it steady. They felt dry and flaky under my hands. "Careful, Felix, hold her steady," he shouted down to me.

"That boy can't hold up a big fellow like you, Walter. Move

over, Felix." George Williams, our neighbour, ambled into our yard smelling of pipe tobacco. I fervently wished George would amble on back before he read our sign, but Father was delighted.

"Oh, hello, George. Thanks."

"What you nailing up there, Walter?" George wore carpenter's pants every day except Sunday. He pressed his ample belly against the ladder. "I'm used to holding ladders, Felix. She won't budge now." George was the volunteer fire chief.

"It's a sign, George, a sign," Father shouted down.

George leaned back from the ladder and looked up. "God dam Smallwood." His thick lips formed the words slowly. Then, his hand flew away from the ladder as if it were hot. I grabbed it tighter in case he'd try to kick it out from under Father.

George turned his lined face up toward Father. He spoke slowly, as if he were dictating to a moron: "Joseph R. Smallwood is the greatest man who ever lived in Newfoundland, except for Jesus Christ."

"Jesus Christ never lived in Newfoundland," said Father, missing the point as usual.

Recovering from shock and anger, George tried again. "Walter, I should haul you down off that ladder and beat the living blazes out of you."

Father stopped hammering.

George went on, "Why are you so down on Mr. Smallwood?"

"Just that he's trying to kill a way of life, that's all, George."

"Joseph R. Smallwood brought us, on this godforsaken

rock, into Canada. I don't have to tell you that, Walter. You're from the mainland! He took us from starvation and the dole to the baby bonus and old-age pensions."

Father did not flinch on the top of his rickety ladder. "That doesn't change a thing. Did you ever hear of resettlement? Resettlement, George? That's what Joe Smallwood and his government are doing to hundreds of our small communities."

"Small communities? What's that got to do with you, Walter? Curlew is not being resettled. Sure, you're not even a Newfoundlander."

Father climbed down, his hammer in his hand. I'd seen him knock down a man once, and he was always punching the heavy bag that he hung in the stable. But he just stood at the foot of the ladder.

"You're welcome to your opinion, George. There's mine." He pointed the hammer up to the sign, looking as righteous as Moses who had just chiselled his own commandments.

George looked at him for a long moment, and then he lowered his eyes to the ground. "There's nothing else to be said." He turned and walked the few steps back to his own yard, quietly closing the wooden gate behind him.

We watched him go, and we stood for a while at the foot of the ladder. A cool spring wind blew in from the ocean that lay less than a mile away. I shivered in my light shirt.

Father looked at me. "What do you think of my sign, Felix?"

I knew a lot depended on my answer. Finally I said, "You spelled 'damn' wrong."

We both looked up at the sign. "Well, too late to change it now. I hope that's the worst they'll say against it."

It wasn't.

In the house, Shirley was still upset. She was a pretty woman with dark hair that came in loose curls to her shoulders. She had heard the nails going into the house and must have felt the pain of each one.

"Your supper is ready," she said.

We ate hash silently until she asked, "What did you nail to the front of the house?"

"A sign."

"What kind of sign?"

"A political sign."

"What does it say?"

Father looked up from his corned beef hash and laid down his fork. "It says 'God dam Smallwood.'"

Father looked unmoved, though he must have seen her wince, too.

"How long will you be leaving it on the house?"

"I don't know. But I'll have a serious problem if you tell me to take it down."

"Will you take it down if I tell you to?" she asked.

Father was stumped. He looked down and searched for the answer in his hash.

"Why would you tell me to do that?"

"Because it will affect everyone who lives in this house. It will affect me and Felix at school. The premier is a very powerful man."

"Powerful? This is Canada, Shirley, not Russia. We are all free here. We have free speech. I can say what I want, can't I?"

"You can say it, but we'll all pay for it. We'll get it from the neighbours. You know they all voted Liberal in the last election."

"Sure! When they saw what a government member could get for them. But they were all Conservatives in 1949."

"That doesn't matter. They all claim to be Liberal now, and they won't tolerate an insult like that to Premier Smallwood."

I watched him settle into stubbornness. I'd seen it before. Father was one of those people they put on a rack in the Middle Ages and stretched till he broke into two. But he would never give in, even if the argument was only about the time of day.

"I'll have trouble getting a teaching job this fall. One phone call to the school superintendent and my application gets ignored," she said.

Father was quiet now.

"And what about Felix? He has to walk out from under that sign and go to school every morning. The other kids will ridicule him. This is not Alberta, Walter. People don't put up signs like that in a Newfoundland outport. There are three of us in this house, and you don't make a majority."

Father looked over at me. "What do you say, Felix?"

I looked up at my father, who was no longer chewing his hash. His whole plan was waiting for my answer. Our old tin clock ticked away behind me.

He laid his fork down on the table. "Up or down?" he asked very clearly.

Usually, I ducked this sort of question or waited until someone else started talking. I looked at him, looked at her, and finally said: "I kind of like it."

Father turned his best poker face to Shirley. "There!"

"Would you have taken it down?" she asked.

"Yes," he said, and continued eating his hash.

I believed him.

"I am the minority, as usual," she said. Father and I ate our hash quietly. She got up to steep tea. "I hope we're all ready to pay the price for it." Shirley had more sense than the two of us, but she was not my real mother, so I always sided with him. Unfair as that might be.

The next day the school bus did a strange thing. Instead of stopping down the road, it stopped right in front of our house. Sam, the driver, had the window down, and I could see him looking up at the sign, mouthing it over and over. Then the penny dropped in his head and a long whistle came out of him. I looked up and saw everyone crowded onto our side of the bus, which brought her down on her starboard springs. After a few titters, a guffaw, and a stifled chortle or two, the whole bus erupted into shouts and laughter. It rocked, and I thought it might tip over.

When I got on, I could smell the beer on Sam's breath, even at eight o'clock in the morning. "Hey, Felix! The election ain't for another two years," he teased.

Two or three older girls sitting up front kept laughing, but I was not ashamed. I was almost famous, and I was proud of Father, even if he was a nut from Canada.

At school, the news of our sign mingled and merged with the other big stories of the morning: Billy Walters had found a condom behind the school. Joyce Dithers was pregnant, again. Freddy Jones's dad had tried to kidnap him, again.

"Dad mustn't know our Freddy very well," Tammy Fagan said to a laughing crowd. Biggest news of all was that Dipsky was traded to the Leafs. "Year of the Leafs! Year of the Leafs," chanted Monk, alone. No one would join Monk if he chanted, Free chips and Coke.

Later, at recess, I went into the library, passing under Victoria's sign, WE ARE SMALLWOOD AND WE SHALL NOT BE BEAT. Monk was sitting alone, in his white shirt and tie; you never needed an appointment to see Monk.

"Hey, Felix! I heard you've gone into politics," he whispered.

I said nothing, but sat beside him and opened a book.

"Lot of Liberals around here, you know," he added.

"It's my father."

"I figured that. He sounds as weird as mine. I think it's a mainland thing."

"That's the part that really kills me. He's not even a Newfoundlander, so why does he care about Smallwood?"

Monk thought for a moment, and then said, "It's called overcompensation. He feels he has to be even more of a Newfoundlander than the locals."

I could only shake my head.

"The kids won't hassle you for a while. Then their parents will start talking it up around the kitchen tables. Soon you'll be up to your ass in trouble. When that happens, I don't know you!"

"That doesn't seem fair."

"Felix, you're lucky to be getting along with those kids at all. You're bookish and odd, like me. On top of that, your father is a mainlander. It's a wonder anyone speaks to you."

A lock of thick hair fell over his glasses. His lips were fat, but well-formed. Four fat fingers and a thumb brushed back the fine hair.

Then, Monk looked toward the door, and Ellen Monteau floated into the library. She wore a pink cashmere sweater, and her hair was held up in the back by a pink ribbon. Indifferent to the glances of boys and the whispers of girls, she came directly to our table. I got up to leave, thinking she was there to consult Monk.

"Felix," said the voice from Tara. "Do you have a sign on your house damning Mr. Smallwood?"

"Yes," a strange voice croaked.

"That took courage. Your family must be ready to endure a lot to put up such a sign."

"Thank you, Ellen." I beamed and extended myself to my full five feet two inches.

"My mother and I have always been Conservatives," she added quietly, glanced briefly at Monk, then turned and floated over to the card catalogue.

Conservatives, I thought. She was a Conservative. Then I wanted to be a Conservative, supposing it meant circumcision and blood sacrifice. The old Tory party had changed in my mind from dusty grey to royal blue, the blue of robins' eggs, summer skies, and babies' eyes.

Monk's voice brought me back to reality. "I can see the way your mind is working, Felix, and I have to say *calm down*."

Three girls came and sat at the table in front of us. "There she is." Grace Rodden poked Victoria. "Over by herself at the card catalogue."

"Thinks she's a queen or something big," said Tammy Fagan.

"I love her sweater," Victoria said.

"She wears it every day, for God's sake," Grace said.

"Probably the only one she's got," Fagan said.

"Let's find out," Grace said, and took apart her ballpoint pen with a few quick twists. She tapped out the refill and broke off the nib against the table. Then she put it back into the pen before it leaked too much. She went to the card catalogue and stood beside Ellen. She opened the card drawer with one hand, and with the other, she touched the leaking pen against Ellen's pink sleeve.

Monk and I watched as the blue line spread through the delicate cashmere of Ellen's left sleeve. She looked up and Grace said, "Sorry, my pen must have leaked."

Ellen looked down at her sweater. She lifted the afflicted arm as if she had been wounded. Her books slid to the floor as she fled the library.

"Tap water won't get *that* out. We'll see what she wears tomorrow," Grace said. She turned to glare at me. I looked away.

The next day, Ellen was absent from school. When she did attend the day after, she wore a plain white blouse with a small black ribbon around her neck, like a little tie. It was simple and tasteful, but she no longer walked like the lady from Tara.

I saw her in the hall waiting for class, and I did something very unusual for me. I made a decision. I walked up to her. She looked at me, but I was not frightened this time.

"Methyl alcohol takes out printer's ink," I said.

"Are you sure?" Her hand reached out to my arm for a second.

"My father told me. He used to be a printer."

"It's my mother's only . . . I mean her best . . . sweater."

"Dab it on with a cloth and then just wash it out."

"Thanks, Felix," she said. I walked away with a slight swagger, just like I'd seen Roy Rogers do on TV.

The big game was set to start at eight o'clock, ending with a dance for both schools. The early buses arrived at seven o'clock, and most of us arrived with them. We said we wanted to get good seats, but once inside, we didn't sit. Rather, we milled around the gym in large concentric circles, like schools of sardines, sharing the excitement with our friends. We were keen when the Argentia buses arrived with their kids and their basketball team, last year's champs.

Our girls waited excitedly to see the Argentia boys, and our boys waited to see the Argentia girls. The place reeked of juvenile hormones.

But we grade nines were there for the game! We itched to see the Argentia basketball team and the three new guys from the American naval base. I had never seen an American before.

We rushed out to the parking lot when their buses arrived. The team got off last, and among them were three tall fellows with drawling American accents.

"Hi!" one of them said politely enough to a bunch of our girls, who embarrassed us by cooing and squeaking. Their whole team laughed.

I was standing by the left doorpost leading into the gym, and Monk was leaning against the right one. Inside we could hear the sound of laughing and chattering, and heads pressed together in furtive whispers. The beautiful people—mostly high school girls—sauntered around the gym, ignoring everyone else and greeting one another.

No one talked to Monk or me. We wouldn't even speak to each other if we could help it. At Smallwood, we were rated below the janitors and barely above teachers. We stood like two statues representing the social outcasts a school was *not* supposed to produce.

The Americans were good, but one guy on their team, a physical genius, half boy, half gazelle, and half hummingbird, outdid them all. He could jump into the air and float. Everyone else seemed to fall back to the yellowed hardwood as he stayed aloft, neatly lobbing the ball into our basket. Time and again, it left his hand and sailed over a forest of waving arms in a perfect arc to the swooshing basket. Smallwood slipped further and further behind.

I turned to Monk. His fingers laced, his hands resting on his large belly as he leaned back against the doorpost. "What's his name?"

"Dean Ringley."

"He's some friggin' good, eh?"

"He's the best," said Monk.

Our team was outclassed, except for Jeff Williams. He got

his thirty points, and he never appeared daunted. Most of his teammates did, especially after the first half, with the score sixty to thirty-nine. A few of our guys became chippy, and one gave Dean Ringley an elbow across the teeth. One of their big guys laid a hand on the offender's jersey and said something we couldn't hear. No one touched Ringley for the rest of the game.

So Monk and I stood at our pillories under the red exit sign. The sign could have read CONDEMNED or DAMN FELIX AND MONK, like Father's.

Tammy Fagan whispered in my ear, "I love Joey Smallwood, and I want to have his baby." I could smell her bubble gum, which she blew and popped in my face before swaggering out of the gym. A pimple-faced guy held her hand, looking back at me and smirking.

Later, I walked outside and left Monk to hold up the lintel alone. Smokers clumped behind the buses, and young lovers nestled against the brick walls behind the school. Other more worldly couples wandered into the deep grass beyond.

I was not part of that world, either. I went back inside the gym in time to see Victoria Spaulding leading the cheerleaders in a frantic, last-ditch attempt to rally our sagging team. Game over!

The dance soon followed. Most of the lovers, who had not already reached the high grass, came back in to dance the slow numbers. Some of the Argentia team came refreshed from the showers and found girls. They were in a strange school, high on victory, and indifferent to our critical looks.

Before long, they were asking the girls to dance the jive, the twist, and the waltzes, too. We watched like jealous crows in a grove of eagles.

Monk and I dutifully served as doorposts. When his father walked by, Monk pretended not to see him. I was also relieved he didn't stop to talk, but he proceeded to chat with the suck-ups.

Tammy and Pimples sauntered back in. Both ignored me. Pimples had a large hickey on his scrawny neck, a badge of honour. Eventually, I wandered back out to the parking lot, trying to make sense of the bad news: our loss to Argentia, their stars dancing with our girls, and my spending the evening as a door jamb. My poor father and his doomed sign was in the back of my mind.

As I passed the Argentia bus, I heard low whispers followed by giggles. I put my ear to the emergency door at the back.

Silence.

"So, why are we here?" a male voice asked. Then came a rustle of clothes and a scrabble of feet heading to the front of the bus. I bobbed my head to the side windows to see, but it was too dark and I was too short. The bus door swung open, and a blonde head emerged. From the road behind me, car lights illuminated her for a moment. Her hair was dishevelled, and she blinked into the light like a rock star at Heathrow. Carrying her shoes, she hurried across the parking lot to the school door.

With a shock, I recognized Ellen Monteau.

More steps led to the front of the bus, and a tall figure emerged and shut the bus door. He paused to arrange his hair in the side mirror. I sucked in a deep breath and strolled up to him.

The figure turned to me, startled. As I walked past, I faked my best boyish grin. "Great game! You were terrific!"

"Thanks, kid," said Dean Ringley.

# 2

# Summer

S oon it was summer holidays. Ellen Monteau graduated to
Memorial University, but Curlew was to be my world for
another two years. Summer was a world filled with birds, sun,
hayfields, woods, secret paths, and teenage conspiracies. We
all swam in the ponds and met on the soft evenings by White's
shop and sometimes by the Kissing Rock. We followed wood
paths through scented spruce forests en route to swimming
spots, fishing holes, and secret places. Home for supper and
then back out again until the jewelled sky domed over our
heads.

I traced the two stars on the outside rim of the Big Dip-
per up to Polaris, the North Star, which would guide you
home if you were ever lost. I traced the belt of Perseus, Zeus's
own son, who vanquished the Gorgon, Medusa. My favourite of all was Cassiopeia, the eternal queen upon her throne

of dazzling silver against the backdrop of black eternity. She was easy to spot because she looked like the letter *W* lying on its side.

Years before, my mother had told me we were all made from stardust. Carbon, hydrogen, nitrogen, calcium, phosphorus, magnesium, sodium, sulphur, and chlorine—the elements that make up the human body ever since God created us from the dust of the earth. We are all made from stardust, she said. So, for me, God had no white beard. He was no Charlton Heston telling us to slay the Amalakites. He was more like my mother—loving and wonderful, capable of making the eternal stars. Capable of making Ellen Monteau.

Father's sign stayed on the house. Some mornings he would wipe eggs or cow manure off it, but he did so with a happy heart—a small price to pay for his apostasy.

One day, I came home from swimming with a swollen black eye.

Father was walking from the house to the stable when I came through the gate, and he stopped in mid-stride. "What happened to your eye?"

"Why do you care so friggin' much about Joey Smallwood?" I asked.

We stood in the middle of our yard, under his sign, suddenly equals. "I don't care about Joey Smallwood. I care about our life here in Newfoundland."

The sign shouted over our heads, but we stood silent for another long moment. "When I came here from Alberta, I was tired of life. Tired of the rat race that drove my father into the ground. He was a printer who drank himself to death. And I was a printer repeating his story. So, I took a trip. I was looking for something. I met your mother at Marty's restaurant on Water Street my first day in Newfoundland, and everything changed for me. She was a stranger there, too, at Memorial College. She knew things, she had answers."

I knew *that* was true.

"I fell in love. For me, she was Newfoundland—my new-found chance at life."

"So, she took you out here?"

"Yes, to Delight, where her parents lived."

"Then you should be able to get along with the people here in Curlew! And I shouldn't have this black eye!"

He looked into the distance. "Not necessarily. They'll destroy Newfoundland unless we fight back. Your mother would have fought back."

"Fought for what?"

"The culture of friends, and stories by the fire, and pitching in to help your neighbour. Now it's all about the new TV sets and the Trans-Canada Highway. We'll soon all be alike. Little cut-out imitations of Toronto suburbs. Little puppets dancing to the North American dream. A dream of money and ego. Breathing smog and buying a bigger car, bigger house, bigger, bigger. Trying to impress one another. Then dying."

I put my finger delicately to my eye.

"Come in the house and we'll put a cold compress on your eye. Then I'll teach you how to throw a left hook."

More serious trouble appeared, one July morning, in the person of Wallace Higgins, the police constable from Shipley.

Father opened the door to the tall, uniformed Higgins. In Curlew, you always knew who was at your door before you opened it, because you had just watched them through the kitchen window as they drove up the road and came to your gate. Any arrival was an occasion, but the arrival of an officer of the law was *quite* the occasion, indeed. I watched from the kitchen.

"Yes, Constable Higgins. What can I do for you?" Father asked.

"Mr. Ryan, I have a few questions about your sign." He paused for reaction. "May I come in?"

"No, you may not. Tell me exactly what you want." Father put his hand on the doorpost.

"Walter, we're getting heat from the premier's office. Complaints have been going in from your neighbours. People want the sign down."

"Am I breaking any law?"

"I don't know. I haven't looked into it. I just came to explain the problem to you. It's been up on your house over a month, now. Your point's been made."

"That sign will stay up until I take it down."

"Aren't you being a little . . ." He searched for a non-offensive word. "Stubborn?"

"Yes, sir, I certainly am, as is my perfect right. I can be as stubborn as I wish about the signs I put on my house. My neighbours are free to do the same. They can put hosannas to Joe Smallwood on their houses if they like."

"Let's say you can, and now you've done it. There's no need to rub it in."

"I know your position in this, Wallace. You're doing the dirty work for other people. Sorry, the answer is no."

"Good day, Walter."

"Good day, Constable."

No more to it than that. The dignified Higgins formally closed the gate and got back into his squad car. He turned around in the road without rising dust. I saw him take off his hat and place it on the seat beside him as he drove away. Shirley looked out the kitchen window as his cruiser disappeared down the road like a ship of hope departing the wharf. She went to the stove and put the kettle on. "You want some tea, Felix?"

"No, thanks."

"Me neither," she said, and pushed the kettle to the back of the stove.

I stood by the kitchen door when Father came into the room. Shirley rinsed the dishes and put them in the drying rack. He came over to the sink, took the towel, and began drying the dishes. Finally, she said, "It will soon get a lot worse."

Later that morning, I ran over to White's shop, where I helped out to earn pocket money. It was the only shop in Curlew. We used to buy everything there before the supermarket opened in Shipley. The Whites liked me because I was quiet and did my work without comment. I walked under the big sign, WHITE'S GENERAL STORE, to find Clara behind the counter. She looked up and grunted. She must have been in a good mood.

"Heard you had visitors, today," she remarked as she wrapped a pound of sliced bologna in waxed paper.

No question was posed, so I offered no answer.

There had been no clock allowed in the shop since the time of her late husband. Old Wayne White had decided a clock would encourage employees to be clock-watchers.

I always began sweeping the shop before the customers arrived. After that, I would restock the shelves and then sweep out the storeroom. When I came back and began sweeping the main shop, Clara said, "I guess it was about the sign your father nailed to the house."

I stopped sweeping.

"Bound to cause concern," she explained in the self-indulgent, muttering way old people can get away with.

My broom was still. One bad word about Father and that broom was going across the floor and I was going home. She could do her own friggin' sweeping.

"Your father never . . ." Then our eyes met. Boom! She saw the fire.

She laid down her bologna.

"Come here," she beckoned with a bony finger. I put my broom flat on the floor and joined her behind the counter. It was like centre stage in a theatre, and I was a backstage person at best.

She took my arm in her mummified old claw and led me to the big front window. "See that new paved road, Felix? See that road? Joe Smallwood put that road there. Look at it!"

I looked and saw the black tarmac line running through our community like a bright new scar. Her grip tightened on my arm.

"See the new cars on it? Do you know where they're going? They're going to goddamn Shipley to buy groceries, that's where they're going."

Her lips snarled back over yellow teeth.

"Do you have any idea what that road did to our business? Destroyed it! Killed poor Wayne! We used to have a business here, Felix." She let go of me and raised both of her arms in the air, indicating the shop around her. I stepped back.

"We were a general dealer, not a grocer. We sold people everything they needed to live, boy, from the bed they were born in to the board for the box they were buried in. They bought their Christmas gifts here; they clothed their children here; we even sold books. Books, Felix, books, not to speak of tons of coal, canvas for their floors, felt for their roofs. Some of them never paid us, never will."

She paused and sighed.

"All that ended because of Joey's road. It took them to the supermarket in Shipley. They took their money with them; only came here when they wanted to 'charge it.' Wayne would stand here and watch the cars headed for Shipley. He'd look over this counter at the empty shop, and he'd cry! I saw that big man cry, Felix."

Her frail body leaned back against the wall, her arms stretched out as if she were being crucified to the shelves of shaving lotion and hairspray.

Then she came down from her cross and hunched closer to me. I could smell her lilac bath oil. Her thin grin suggested another terrible secret. She glanced out the window and around the empty shop, then put her mummified arm around my neck and whispered, "Do you know what Wayne's last words were?"

I surely didn't, but continued to stare at her.

"'Goddamn Joey Smallwood' were the last words that passed his lips. He said them to me many times before." Her eyebrows rose, and she looked quickly around the shop again. "All our customers were Liberals, and Wayne knew they wouldn't shop here at all if they heard him say such a thing. He never spoke up, but those were his last words on this earth."

A can of hairspray fell behind her with a tinny clang and rolled across the floor. She recovered herself and pronounced her next words very clearly. "I hope your father never takes it down!"

Silence filled the shop. A car drove past on Joey's pavement. Then, even that sound faded away, as Clara looked off into space.

"Now finish your sweeping," she said. I went around the counter and picked up my broom. She began to rearrange the shelves.

The door opened with a ring of the tiny bell. "Good morning, Mrs. White," said Doris Lyons.

A customer! Showtime! "Good morning, Doris," said the old matron. "What can I do for you this morning?"

"Just a few things for the garden party salad. Have you any fresh lettuce?"

"A fresh box just in. Dick hasn't even got it unpacked yet. Send one of your boys down later this afternoon."

"Then I'll take a dozen eggs and some sliced bread, and a couple of packs of Freshie. They drink it like water," said Doris with one of her easy laughs. Old Clara liked Doris because she had remained a loyal customer in spite of the Shipley supermarket.

After I swept the floor, I went out to the old warehouse with an empty carton to restock the shelves. The doors were open, and I heard a grunting noise ahead of me. The lights were never on in the daytime, and the place had a cool, dim feel. It carried the accumulated smells of fifty years of commerce: a hint of dried peas from the mainland, the tang of molasses that had ruptured perhaps thirty years ago, the musk of potatoes that hadn't made it to market. The semi-darkness suddenly reminded me of the Argentia team bus in the darkened parking lot.

I saw Dick White, Clara and Wayne's only son, opening a box of lettuce with a claw-bar. Dick was about forty-five with a youthfulness that sheltered, unmarried men often retain—an immaturity in both appearance and world view.

His hair was short, curly, and still black. It had never been thick, and he coiffed it straight by combing it close to his head. The tight little curls refused to be stretched into straight lines, without the aid of gels and greases, but Dick persisted. Brylcreem was his ally in this unending struggle. Dick's smell was the sweet, oily smell of Brylcreem.

The rest of his body was as youthful as his hair. He was slight and slim without the rigours of regular exercise, and he had a small upturned nose.

"F-F-Felix?" he said in his slight stutter. "Are you stocking the sh-sh-shelves? Good boy!" He continued to tug at the box, grunting and sweating until finally popping the wire bracket on the wooden crate.

In the days that followed, I realized something was wrong between Clara and Dick. They never let me hear anything, of course, but I occasionally noticed a grumble, a cold look, or a silence that Monk would call "pregnant."

Then, one Monday morning when I strolled in for work, I saw a shiny new white convertible at the end of their long driveway.

"See my new car?" asked Dick. "She's a b-b-beauty. When Mom comes out, I'll take you for a r-r-ride."

And so he did. Clara took her time coming from the house to the shop these mornings. Like she was protesting something. Work to rule. Dick pretended not to notice.

The car was breathtaking. The interior was all leather in a dusty rose colour, almost feminine. Dick sat behind the wheel and set the big eight-cylinder engine varooming. He checked in the rear-view and slicked back his Brylcreemed hair. Then he backed the car onto the road.

It was a hot morning in July 1966, just like the morning when Dick was killed, but on that day he was far from dying. He was showing off his new convertible, not just to the boy who worked for them, but to the whole community.

We rocketed down Joey's road as Dick got the feel of the powerful four-barrel carburetor. It was like a four-wheel generating station that Mr. Chrysler had cleverly made to look like a car. Its raw horsepower threatened to zoom us to unheard-of speeds, perhaps into orbit with Alan Shepard and Uri Gagarin.

All things were possible, that July morning, as I sped around Curlew in Dick White's new car.

Few people were on the road at that hour, but we waved to them all. Dick inspired an air of youthful joy. He was far from a James Dean or a Marlon Brando by contemporary standards, but, at forty-five, Dick was the closest thing to a youthful rebel I had ever seen.

Ahead loomed my father's ominous sign. We passed it silently. I thought I saw Shirley in the yard, but could not be sure because I was not used to travelling at speeds in excess of thirty miles per hour. We hurtled recklessly through the warm summer air. On either side of us, black spruce wafted their scented hosannas as we shot past to the end of the town a mile from the Kissing Rock.

A heady Dick returned us to the store. I thanked him and went back to work bringing stock downstairs from the storage room above the warehouse. Upstairs were stored boxes of pickles, jams, beets, mustard, and ketchup, twelve or twenty-four jars in each cardboard box. Other boxes contained apple juice, tinned fruit, baby food, and molasses. Years ago, the second floor had been a clothing department. Some old baby clothes and women's dresses, unpopular even in the 1950s, remained. Once, I came upon an old pair of lace-up ladies' shoes. In spite of all the leather and lace holes, they were small and delicate.

I was in the process of bringing down a box of twenty-four glass jars of olives when I heard strained voices below. Old Clara hissed angrily, "You can do better than one of the local girls. She's barely out of school. They live in a trailer on a back road.

She was born out of wedlock." My steps slowed at the top of the stair. "She came from nothing, and she will always be nothing!" I could almost see her spit flying through those yellow horse teeth.

"Mother, I t-t-told you I'm only interested in one girl, and that g-g-girl is Ellen Monteau."

At those last two words I lost my footing and toppled against the railing. I caught myself, but the olives were not so lucky. At first, the box arched gracefully over the railing into thin air. Downwards they fell for what seemed like five minutes toward the concrete floor and the two agitated people standing on it. I had opened the carton to stock the shelves. Some bottles hit the floor before the main cargo. Vacuum-packed, they smashed with loud and dangerous explosion of olives, vinegar, and glass.

Clara shrieked and ran back into the shop. A shard of glass cut Dick's shin.

I was cleaning up for the rest of the day. We found olives everywhere. Several had attached themselves to the ceiling, and others to the windows. We found olives upstairs beyond where I had been standing. We even found them in the shop, and they would've had to bounce off four walls to get there.

That evening I walked home with a sick feeling in my stomach, but it had nothing to do with broken glass. "Ellen Monteau" had been the last two words I heard before the Attack of the Olives.

I was repulsed by the thought of Ellen in the arms of a mere mortal like Dick White. She, it seemed to me, deserved a king, a shah, a raja, or, failing these, me. But not Dick White.

At home, things were as crazy as ever. Shirley greeted me in a distracted way in a sleeveless white cotton blouse with little red roses all over it. Soon after I arrived, Father came back in from the stable, where he had been salting hay, and she held out a letter to him. "This came for me in today's mail," she said. In her pretty top and jeans, she looked much younger than Father.

He smelled of hay dust as he wiped the coarse salt from his hands and took the letter without a word. He sat at the kitchen table to read it. Then he looked out the window. "I'm sorry, Shirley."

"What is it?" I asked.

Father began to read. "Dear Mrs. Ryan."

"Walter! Not in front of Felix."

"He's not a boy now, Shirley. He should know what's going on here."

He continued to read.

"We have reviewed your application for the position of grade two classroom teacher at Curlew Elementary. Unfortunately, we find your qualifications unacceptable for the position. Yours truly, John Sutton, District Superintendent, Denominational School System."

He paused for a moment, then observed, "Weren't they the same qualifications you had last year?"

"Yes, but I'm just a term contract. They have to rehire me each year."

"They've done that for the past seven years. There should be a law against this."

"That hardly matters now, does it?"

Supper was a sombre affair. The old tin clock ticked on the warming oven of the cast-iron stove. Father fidgeted with his baked beans, a thick piece of homemade bread lying forgotten by his plate. Shirley sat stiff-backed and ate.

"I should go out to the union office this week," Father said. "There may be some construction going up before the winter."

Shirley looked over at him with some sympathy. "It'll be a hard winter for all of us."

Our gloom was interrupted by a clear double knock on the front door. We looked at each other in surprise. No one used the front door, even in summer. The last person to use it was young Wally Foster to surprise everyone in a game of hide-and-seek. We were all hiding behind the house, and seeing him come through the squeaking front door was like seeing him walk through a wall. He caught us all and won the game.

Father recovered first and went down the hall. I rose and followed. He creaked and squeaked open the thick old door with both hands, and we peered out. Standing on our front step was a smiling, tanned gentleman in a light blue suit. He looked like a movie star with his black, slicked-back hair. He spoke with an American accent, yet somehow formally: "How do you do?"

"Fine, thank you," my father answered.

"Ah am the Reverend John Stone from Church of the Saints in Shipley."

We looked at him blankly.

"May ah come in?"

"Of course, Reverend. Come in," said Father. "Shirley, it's Reverend Stone, from Shipley."

Shirley did not rise from the table.

The reverend swept into the kitchen like a man on a mission. His hat was in his hand, held by long pink fingers. It was light brown felt with a soft look to it. The hatband was blue to match his suit. There was a pink cleanliness about him that filled the room. He looked as if he had travelled here by bathtub, stopping only to slip into his powder-blue suit.

He placed the hat on my chair. "May ah sit?" Without waiting for an answer, he sat in Father's chair. So, Father and I stood, and Shirley sat as we listened to Reverend Stone.

He was an eloquent speaker with a resonant voice couched in his pleasing drawl. He spoke like a man used to speaking. He sat on the chair as if he were posing for a picture, feet flat on the floor, chair turned to face us.

"Ah am here regarding your sign," he began. "People in my flock are concerned about the wording you have chosen to nail to your house and thus put on public display." The tanned face of a thousand American suns dimmed slightly, and a frown touched his pink lips and blue eyes.

"Your whole flock is Liberal?" Father asked (as usual in the wrong church and the wrong pew).

Shirley sat in her chair and looked at the man with the angelic voice. He ignored her and spoke to Father, occasionally looking at me.

"No, no, Mr. Ryan. It has nothing to do with political affiliations. We leave that to the kingdom of man."

"What, then?"

"The word—" he looked at Shirley. "Excuse me, ma'am. The word 'damn' appears in your sign," he said to father.

"So what?"

"Only God can damn to eternal hellfires, Mr. Ryan. You know that."

"Then, what's the problem?"

"It is an affront to God's will that man should use such a profane word. To suggest eternal damnation for anyone is an abomination to the will of God."

Suddenly, Father understood in a flash of revelation what the reverend was talking about. "Are you telling me I should take down my sign because it's God's will?" he asked, still calm.

The reverend chuckled. "Let us just say the word of your sign is an insult to God and to His people."

"You object to the sign on religious grounds?"

"That is correct."

Father's fists clenched, and I noticed a white patch spread around his knuckles and up his hand, almost to the wrist. "The sign stays up," he croaked.

The reverend stood up. He was a tall man. "We begin with a modest request, one Christian to another. But I want you to know we will commence legal proceedings against you on the grounds of obscenity."

"Obscenity?"

"You will be hearing from our lawyers, Metcalf and Mc-Cann."

Taking his hat from my chair, Reverend Stone held it like a theatre prop, turning it lightly in his slender, pink hands. White teeth gleamed, and he smiled at us. "Mrs. Ryan, young man, Mr. Ryan, I wish you all a good day." Then he turned and went back through the front door as if beaming up to another planet. But something about him frightened me. He looked and sounded so charming, but his message was chilling.

Father went to the front door and locked it. We all returned to our cold suppers. The old tin clock ticked away, leading us through time and deeper into gloom.

# 3

# Marriage

Dick was putting his new convertible to good use. He and Ellen were often seen driving up and down the road through the community.

That fall, Dick and Ellen attended the parish Halloween dance, the Christmas concert and dance, the Easter concert (no dance), and the July garden party and dance. Then, in late July, we all got invitations to the August 15 wedding.

I still thought she should marry a shah, a count, a Montreal Canadiens hockey player, or, as I said before, me, but certainly not Dick White. It seemed to me that when God created this world, He did not intend Ellen to marry Dick White.

Once again, Clara and I agreed, but for opposite reasons.

One day, I was sitting on the grass in the shade of the flour store, eating my lunch: a bottle of Orange Crush and an apple flip. The flour store was the largest of the storage sheds, holding one-hundred-pound bags of Robin Hood flour, burlap bags of oats, and rolls of floor canvas.

I heard Clara and Dick arguing down at the house: "You're going to marry *her*?" Clara screamed across the yard. The light wind muffled and carried words to me disjointedly, but "out of my will" and "leave you both nothing" rang out. I stopped chewing on my flip to hear Dick's reply. No wind interposed as he said, "I love the girl, and I will marry her. Do what you like with the business and the land."

I liked Dick after that. I ate my apple flip, feeling better about the whole deal. Somehow, he now seemed more worthy of Ellen Monteau. Clara never relented. Every morning when I came to work, Dick would be tending the shop alone. His mother would not turn up till well after eleven.

It was a big wedding by our standards. I was invited. Shirley and Father were invited. It was a grand church affair with most of the community in attendance. Ellen looked stunning, of course. She glowed under the translucent wedding veil with the softness of the Madonna.

Clara would not stand in the reception line, claiming the prerogative of old age. I had often seen her stand behind the counter for eight hours, but she was fighting this marriage right down to, and past, the wire.

The meal was as fine as the Ladies Auxiliary had ever prepared, and the speeches were as boring as the gentlemen had ever presented. Soon after, the bar opened and the band started. Some business friends of old Wayne had turned up from St. John's. They were rich, tanned, and dressed in flashy clothes. Their wives were apparitions of wrinkled skin and ostentatious jewels of the tacky rich. They laughed and danced among themselves and pretty much ignored the rest of us. They left early.

Clara sat awkwardly at the head table, smiling ever so thinly when necessity dictated. Dick asked her to dance once, but she refused. He and Ellen danced. I was amazed Dick knew how. Ellen's white heels clicked and floated over the floor. Each lovely curve of her was enveloped by the white wedding dress. Sigh.

Her mother and her mother's boyfriend, Gerald, sat at one table—a little island of drama. There were no other guests from her side of the family. Maud Monteau had once been gorgeous, and she still carried a weary charm. Her eyes were tired but icy green. She wore makeup and looked pretty good, though not dressed with any great style or expense. She was drinking a lot, and so was her boyfriend. They danced occasionally in the early evening. But for the most part they offered little attention to each other, concentrating instead on the drinks in front of them and the dancing couples on the floor.

Dick came over and asked Maud for a dance. She smiled and grandly offered him her hand. They danced once.

Equally isolated were Father and Shirley, who sat alone at a large table. I went over to join them soon after the band started.

Father did not drink or smoke or dance. He sat and looked at the band, in which he had about as much interest as in going to the moon. Shirley was sipping a Bacardi and Coke. In the centre of their table glowed a newly lit cigarette in a square glass ashtray.

I sat beside them, and Father turned to me. "Felix, how are you?" he asked, somewhat formally. Not much else to say.

We had very few friends in Curlew since Father's sign had gone up. We sat abandoned in a sea of conviviality that grew and swirled around us.

Liberal opposition to Father's rudeness, if not his vulgarity, was growing steadily. Some were polite about it, but others were not. As the night and the drinking continued, Father could well expect a beer bottle in the head or a well-chosen insult.

So we sat silently. Father looked straight ahead. Shirley sipped her drink, a spurned cigarette billowing plumes of grey smoke straight up, marking us as the blighted table. I knew she didn't want to smoke it in front of me. She was always trying to be my real mother and set a good example. Suddenly, it touched me that she would let her cigarette, which she obviously enjoyed, burn away in the middle of our table. I wanted to tell her it was okay for her to smoke it, but then she would have to admit it was hers. So, we all said nothing as the cigarette burned down to the filter and died.

I looked over toward the bar and saw Monk. "I'll be back later," I said to Father, like a soldier in Custer's 7th Cavalry sneaking away from the Little Bighorn.

Monk had a glass in his hand. He was smiling broadly, but did not speak.

"What are you doing, Monk?"

"Having a little drink of rum, Felix, my lad," he said grandly.

"But the bartender wouldn't sell rum to you."

"Quite right. I didn't buy it, I stole it."

"What?"

"They never notice after a few drinks. You only steal from the drunks. Want to try one?"

"I never drank liquor in my life."

"Then tonight's your big night, my friend. What would you like? I'm a Scotch drinker, myself, but this is all I could find."

"I don't know," I said.

Monk slipped nimbly around the bar. He was soon back with two glasses of dark liquid. The smell suggested they were not Coke.

"Rum was all I could get. You Newfies are not very sophisticated drinkers. Ever hear of Scotch?" He held one of the glasses out to me.

I took the offered glass and held it to my nose. It smelled like molasses mixed with kerosene.

"You take it through the mouth, Felix, not the nose. Ha! You're confusing it with snuff."

He took a gulp of his own. Then I took a gulp of mine.

The taste was predictably horrible, but a gently tingling numbness pervaded my mouth and throat. There was also the satisfaction of accomplishing the feat without throwing up. As well, there was a warm feeling of secret conspiracy, even if it was with Monk.

I took another sip and smiled. It was almost tolerable. I put my elbow up on the bar as I had seen some of the men do. It was difficult, for the bar was level with my ear.

"Not bad, eh?" I heard a voice say. It was Monk. He was now standing at the far end of a distant bar, about two miles away. Then he fluttered back into focus.

"No," I heard myself say. "Not bad at all." He handed me another.

"They're not full because you have to let them have a few sips before you steal them."

He headed off to the other end of the bar, where the bartender and four men were huddled together in animated conversation.

"Hello, Felix." I recognized the voice even before I turned around. Ellen stood over me, a vision in white. Her veil was up and surrounded her face. She smiled. "Are you having a nice time?"

"Yes."

"Would you like to dance?" she asked.

"I don't know how," I mumbled.

"I'll show you. It's called an old-fashioned waltz, so you just count one, two, three, and move your foot with each count."

She dragged me about the floor for five minutes.

"You are a goddess," I said as the dance ended. "And you should have servants tending to your every whim." I had her attention.

She put her hand on my arm. "Felix, you are a dreamer. I used to be, too, but there's no payoff in it." She kissed me gently on the forehead. I think I closed my eyes.

She floated away.

Soon, Monk was back complaining about the rum. He handed me another glass. "By the way," he said, "Cyril Durning is going to kill your father tonight."

"What?" My hand stopped in mid-reach.

He indicated the men with the bartender. "They really got it in for your father." He grinned widely behind his glass and fat fingers. "Something about a sign on your house, Felix. Ha."

"Why's Cyril so mad about Father's sign?"

"He's not. He's just trying to suck in with the Liberals. He was the Conservative campaign manager last election, and now he wants to get back into the fold."

"He wants to kill my father?"

"Doesn't have to actually kill him; a severe beating would suffice."

I looked down the bar and saw Cyril Durning's prematurely bald head and stout neck turning to better view Father. My eyes blurred and then cleared.

"Father knows how to fight really well," I thought aloud.

"They are four plus the bartender," Monk reminded me casually.

Panic seized me. I turned quickly and walked over to Father's table. Shirley and he both smiled as I put my glass on the table and sat between them. Suddenly, they realized I was drinking rum.

Shirley reached for the cigarette, which had been relegated to the ashtray. Father ignored her glare as he turned to me. There was a new look on his face. It was not blame, but appraisal, as if deciding how to handle a new situation.

I was too upset about Cyril Durning to even try to explain my drinking. "Cyril Durning is going to beat you up," I said, and watched the look on his face change again as he tuned in to this second reality. Father loved a crisis. It somehow brought out the best in him. All his foolish ideas evaporated into a fine focus of clarity.

He looked over toward the bar. "When?" he asked softly.

"Tonight. Here."

"Good." He glowed. He pushed his chair back from the table. Shirley kept on smoking. "Shirley, there's going to be some trouble here tonight."

"I know."

"You can leave now."

She took the cigarette away from her lips. "No, I want to stay. At least they won't kill you here."

He sat in silence for a long moment. I loved to watch my father thinking, for that was the only time he was really relaxed. His eyes were distant and his face radiated a new calm, as if he had been waiting for this moment. Then he unbuttoned the top of his shirt and laid his tie on the table. He reached over and put his hand on my arm.

"Thank you for your help, Felix," he said. It was one of the few times I ever remembered him touching me.

He got up and walked toward the bar. Shirley saw the tears in my eyes. She put an arm around my neck and pulled my head onto her shoulder. She took another puff of her cigarette.

"It's the smoke in my eyes," I explained.

"Yes, mine too," she said.

Soon, noise and confusion broke out at the bar. The band, of course, did what all bands do when a disturbance breaks out; they stopped playing, and everyone's attention focused on the racket.

I sniffed back my tears and stood up on my chair. Father was now surrounded. The bartender loomed behind him, and Cyril Durning faced him. Cyril was about forty-five and stocky. His thick neck led up to a bald head. What hair remained grew longish around his ears.

I saw Monk going around to the vacant tables looking for Scotch.

Most of the men were, by this time of evening, in their shirt sleeves. The women were still in their frilly dresses. "Walter Ryan is about to get the beating he deserves," I heard one of them say.

I jumped down and pushed in through the crowd toward the centre of the confusion. Elbows smacked against my ears, but I rudely pushed on through a forest of hips and dangling arms. I could hear Cyril shouting something about Father being from the mainland and shoving his politics on the rest of us.

I emerged immediately behind Cyril Durning. His feet were set well apart, and the strangest parts of his pose were his hands. His fingers were splayed apart in tension as he spoke. The tendons and veins on his hands and arms bulged. His fists were not clenched, and each finger seemed set to attack Father on its own. I could see my father in front of him, not three feet away, and quietly waiting. His feet were a little apart, and his fists were already clenched.

He was looking steadily at Cyril when one of the other men suddenly took a swing at him. The punch missed his jaw and struck him on the collarbone. He toppled back against the padded bar with a grunt and a sudden thud.

At the same instant, Cyril launched himself at Father with a muttered obscenity. The splayed-out fingers of his right hand swung back into my face. I saw his pinky ring glint, and like a cat, my own right hand reached up and grabbed him by that one finger.

He tried to flick me off, and I lost my footing, but as I felt my bum drag the floor, I heard the crack of his finger breaking. He screamed and fell to his knees clutching his hand.

The room went silent except for Cyril kneeling on the floor and groaning over his broken finger.

I looked to Father and saw him punch a fellow in the mouth. The man's head snapped back, his legs gave way, and he slid to the floor. The bartender reached over the bar and wrapped his arms around my father's chest. The fellow who'd struck him earlier moved in with a raised fist that faltered as a loud voice boomed through the room. "Okay! Stop! That's enough!"

The bulky form of Constable Wallace Higgins strolled amidst the brawling men. He looked to the kneeling Cyril, now rocking on his haunches, holding his broken finger and moaning. He looked to the other assailants, and they looked away. He then turned to Father, who was wild-eyed and looking around for someone to take a swing at. Higgins laid a hand on his right arm, and fearing Father's left hook, I closed my eyes. But when I opened them, Higgins was leading him back to our table.

"Something belonging to you, I think, Shirley," he said as he pushed Father into a chair. He looked at me and smiled. Jeez, that Constable Higgins was a nice man.

Father was flushed and beaming. His shirt was open almost to his waist, and he looked ten years younger. "Damn that Higgins," he whispered. "I could have taken 'em all." He looked to me, his eyes dancing with excitement. "How did you take down Cyril Durning?"

"I grabbed hold of his little finger and hung on till it broke."

A smile, then a grin, struck across Father's face. His shoulders shook with quiet laughter and perhaps relief.

I looked past him to see Phil Janes setting Cyril's finger in a temporary splint, then leading him out the door.

Father repeated my words, "I hung on till it broke," then convulsed again with laughter. He reached over and patted me on the shoulder.

"Good for you, Felix. I think I'll have another drink. Care to join me in a Coke? Another Bacardi, Shirley?"

I took the last sip of my rum and watched a sad tear glisten on Shirley's cheek as she looked at Father.

It amazes me that my memories of those days are summer memories. We had our troubles: Shirley and Father had little or no work, and we were exiles in our own land. But. But. But. Those memories are filled with sunshine and shouting and splashing in a pond. At night, stars reigned in a clear sky, and the big sign stood on my father's house, in defiance of God and man.

# 4

# Betrayal

**B**efore long, Dick and Ellen were running the shop. Ellen was also doing some courses at Memorial University, so Dick was left to do most of the work. Old Clara White only came in to slice bologna, bag apples into dozens, and onions into pounds. A new guy was hired in the shop, Joe Gosine. He was the colour of the darkest tan we had ever seen in Curlew, darker even than the Americans. He had just arrived from Lebanon the year before, but things hadn't clicked for him with his relatives on Bell Island, who were diamond jewellers and business people. For unknown reasons, Joe ended up with us.

Joe's job was mainly to shovel coal, the distant cousin of diamonds. Dick had taken to wearing a white shirt and tie in the shop, and shovelling coal was a dirty job. Joe's job was to fill bags with fifty and one hundred pounds of coal.

Sometimes I helped him by holding the bags while he shovelled. It wasn't too bad in the winter or during wet weather, but on a hot, dry summer day, the dust would rise with every movement of shovel or feet. It got in our eyes and our noses, not to mention our clothes and faces. Fortunately, few people in Curlew burned coal in summer.

Joe boarded with the Whites, not in their big old house, but in a two-room apartment built in the flour store. It was cold in winter, but in summer it was warm and pleasant. It radiated past days, and you could almost see old Wayne White coming around a corner with a roll of canvas on his shoulder. The red and black DRINK COCA COLA sign, with the smiling girl, still ran across the flour store door.

I was sweeping out the flour store one day when I found Dick's dolls.

Dick's workroom had always been off limits. He had politely explained that he would be cleaning it up himself, but late one afternoon I saw the light shining from under the door, and I opened it. At one end of the room, which smelled of newly cut wood and fresh paint, was a workbench with several vises attached to its top. On it were dozens of chisels, saws, augers, and woodworking tools of every description.

The rest of the room was filled with dozens of small wooden people, each about three feet high. They were lifelike with flesh and clothing painted on them. Their eyes were wide open, the irises cut round in the wood. Their arms were all down by their sides, and their little feet perched together in pairs on the floor. They looked like people you'd see walking down Joey's paved road. I found ones of Clara, Joe, Shirley, and Father. The most attractive one was of Ellen. I was looking for one like me when

I lost my nerve. As I scurried out the door, I noticed their faces were all smiling—even Clara, who never smiled, looked happy and benign. Dick had created a little Curlew whose citizens were all content with life.

The day Dick was killed was another splendid summer's day. I was the only one in the shop when the robber came in. Dick was out back refilling the salt beef barrel from five-gallon buckets. But a moment after the stranger came through the door, Dick was back behind the counter. Shopkeepers have this sixth sense even without that little bell over the door.

Dick's smile was a question as he spoke to the man. "Yes? Can I help you?"

Any stranger was news in Curlew, but this one was stranger than your average stranger. His collar was up and his cap was hauled down to his eyes. He leaned in over the counter.

"I want all your money, now. And what's in the safe, too." He produced an old army handgun and levelled it at Dick. The picture is etched in my mind, like E. J. Pratt's seagull.

Outdoors, the sun gazed from a blue sky. A light wind moved through the tops of the tallest trees. At 10:00 a.m. the paved road was deserted as the asphalt started to warm up. That morning was about to pass into the lore of local history.

I saw the words US ARMY on the blue metal of the gun. Dick froze. The robber froze. I froze. The three of us waited for Dick's reaction.

Then I noticed the meathook in his right hand. He had

brought the rusty iron hook with him from the salt beef room. I couldn't tell if he even remembered it was still in his hand. Behind the counter, it was almost hidden from the robber.

I am still amazed how clearly my mind was working at the time. I was not a bit frightened after the initial shock. The rising of one eyebrow marked Dick's recovery from his own shock. I knew that his response was now imminent.

In fact, the initial surprise was still partly on his face as he swung the meathook hard at the robber. It seemed to take a long time for the blow to land, for Dick swung the hook up from his side, back behind him, and then down at the robber. The process seemed to take minutes. It really took about a second.

Still, the robber's gun did not go off. The hook struck him in the front of his neck and imbedded there. Blood spurted out of the astonished man. I think Dick was astonished, too. He continued his attack by pulling the robber toward him like a piece of hooked salt beef. As the robber hit the side of the counter, the hook popped out. He slipped to one knee and rested the arm with the gun in it on the counter. Dick and I looked at the gun. Neither of us moved. The robber pulled himself up to his feet and then pushed back from the counter. Blood was pouring from his neck and soaking his black windbreaker. He had just received a fatal wound and looked smaller than before. Then he raised the gun and shot Dick.

One shot. It struck Dick full in the chest, and he tumbled backwards into the shelves. Cans of aerosol deodorant and packages of hairpins fell to the floor as his arms flayed out. Then he turned his back to the robber and me and grasped one of the shelves with his right hand for stability.

It didn't work. Like a wooden doll of Dick White, he slowly toppled to the left. His right hand was stuck out, but unattached to the steadying shelf. He hit the floor with a soft rustle of his starched white coat.

The robber and I looked at each other. I saw the blood still flowing freely from the wound in his neck. He seemed to suddenly remember it, too. He dropped the gun to the floor.

He was only a kid, about eighteen or nineteen. His face turned the colour of ashes. He looked at me again, and his jaw slacked and his eyes rolled around in his head. He turned and sized up the door, like someone about to park a car. He pushed himself toward it. One bloody hand clung to the door frame after his body had passed through. He fell and died not twenty feet from his old car.

A big housefly buzzed across the shop and pitched. On tiptoes, I peered over the counter at Dick. He lay neatly, as if mindful that someone would have to clean up after him.

Ellen and Joe Gosine came through the back door.

"What was the noise?" she asked through full red lips. Then she saw Dick, and her scream jolted me to the horror of what had just happened.

I ran around the stove and in behind the counter. As I passed, an image stayed in my mind to be recalled later: by Ellen's side, almost hidden in the folds of her frilly dress, her long white fingers were knotted tightly with Joe's dark ones.

"My God, Joe!" she shrieked.

Joe let go of her hand, and we looked down at Dick. He was perfectly still, but wheezing slightly. Joe looked at me. "Felix, go get the doctor."

I was out the door in a flash. Doctor Phil Janes was often drunk, but still as fine a doctor as Curlew ever saw. He came immediately, leaving a glass of whisky and his dinner on the table. His cook, Wilma Bartlett, clucked at the inconvenience of it all.

We were both out of breath after we hurried to the shop. A small crowd leaned over the counter, and the family huddled on the floor inside, waiting for the doctor.

Clara was on her knees beside Dick. She was holding a towel against the bullet hole with both hands.

"Easy, Clara," were the first words Doctor Janes spoke as he slipped to his knees beside her. He lifted her hand and the towel and looked at the wound. Then he looked at Clara and saw the desperation in her eyes.

"Let's get to work, now," he said, slipping out of his jacket and tossing it up onto the counter. "Joe, get over here."

"Yes, Doctor."

"Get his shoes off, belt off, pants loose." He was rooting around in his big bag.

"Clara, let go now." She would not, so he gently lifted the old woman away from her stricken son. He took her place at Dick's chest and put a large bandage over the bleeding hole. He spoke to Clara softly: "Go wash the blood off your hands, now. I want you to phone the hospital in Fillmore. Tell them we're on the way and he's lost a lot of blood."

"Will he live?"

"I don't know."

A familiar voice came from beyond the counter. "My truck is just outside." It was Father, and I knew things would be all right now. I believed he could cure all ills, even death itself, such was my faith in him. "Get a mattress from the storage room," Father said.

"I'll get the mattress," said Joe.

"I need someone to sign for me to send him to hospital." Doctor Janes produced a form from his bag. "Where's Clara?"

Ellen pushed forward. "I'll sign it. I'm his wife!"

"Yes, of course," said the doctor, and held it up to her.

Dick's last ride to Fillmore was in the back of Father's Dodge pickup truck.

They brought him back home the next day, a certified corpse, to the Curlew Funeral Home. Then the world of euphemisms took over.

Will Mullins met us all at the door and "took possession" of the "remains." Will was a classic undertaker, tall and lanky with a thick head of dyed-black hair. His tresses were combed back with deep tracks over his ears. He was unctuous and simpering on behalf of the "bereaved." Wringing his long, thin hands, he welcomed us into his "home," the funeral parlour built onto his house.

"Mrs. White." He touched Clara's hand.

"Will," Clara mumbled an acknowledgement.

"Mrs. White," he said again, and Clara look surprised.

But Ellen greeted him clearly. "Mr. Mullins."

He nodded to Joe Gosine and me without really seeing us. Ellen tried to play a wifely role, but it was Clara who picked out the casket from among the five or six on the premises. She chose the most expensive, as we all knew she would. She handed Mullins Dick's good suit, the one in which he had been married. She also gave him a small wrapped package. The others wondered what was in it, but I had seen her wrap Dick's Brylcreem.

Two days later, Dick's funeral was held in the same church where his marriage had been two years before. Much the same crowd was present. Dick looked good. His tight black curls were shining under copious applications of Brylcreem, just as in life.

Ellen was as ravishing in black as she had been in white. A sheer black veil replaced the sheer white one she had worn on her wedding day. When she knelt alone in front of her husband's casket, her lace gloves were clasped in prayer and her head was bowed. She cried a bit on her mother's shoulder, as was appropriate under the circumstances.

Clara was just as stoic at the funeral as she had been at the wedding. But she had noticeably less trouble standing up during the service.

The shop was closed for one day after the funeral, "in deference to the deceased," as Will Mullins put it. I stayed around the house and talked to Shirley. She openly smoked a pack a day now.

"When do you go back to work?" she asked me.

"Monday."

"You're almost a man now." She seemed to be looking through me as she sat at our yellow chrome table and matching chrome chairs with the yellow plastic over the padded backs and seats. July sun shone through the kitchen window.

I leaned my rump against the sink and studied her. "What do you mean?"

"Well, you're the only one in this house with a paying job."

"I guess I am. Does that bother you?"

"Yes, it bothers me when we have to do without things because of your father's sign."

The door opened, and Father came in from tending his sign with a bucket and cloth.

"Eggs?" I asked.

"No, tar this time," he said, and reached under the sink for the bottle of kerosene.

"Are you going back at it, now?" I asked.

"Yes."

So Father and I went out into the yard. I held the ladder as he climbed up to the sign and began cleaning it. Two years older now, and starting to grow, I held the ladder firmly, knowing that no one else would help him. Sun, wind, snow, rain, as well as Liberals, had all assailed his sign. Cleaning it had become a daily ritual, like brushing his teeth.

"She wants it down, doesn't she," he said.

"Yes."

"Soon, I think, soon," he said.

In the two years the sign had been up, his jaw had been broken twice in community altercations. I still have memories of him at the table, drinking soup through a straw, with his jaw wired up.

I held the ladder as he wiped off the black globs with a cloth and some kerosene. He looked smaller than I remembered him as he dabbed and pushed at the black tar defacing his sign. But his jaw was firmly set, as if the wires were still in place.

On Monday, back at my summer job, things were pretty much as usual on the surface. The shop was open, with Clara and Ellen behind the counter. Sometimes, I caught myself looking at Ellen and longing for her, envying Joe Gosine, who could secretly hold her hand. He was usually moving around out back, bringing supplies down from the sheds to the shop and the attached stockroom, much the same job as Dick had formerly done.

Life went on as week followed week, except without Dick.

But I began to notice subtle differences. I was up in the flour store loft sweeping one Saturday in November. It was suppertime, and I had only a little more to do to finish the job, so I worked on. Below me, I heard Joe come in and go to his room.

Then someone else entered the main door, and Joe's door opened and closed again. I went into Dick's workshop and crept over the boards. Muffled voices—Joe's and Ellen's—came from below. Soon the voices stopped and I heard other sounds. The cooing sounds of tenderness and love. My heart was beating out of my chest, so I crept back through the dolls and returned to the shop.

"Did you see Ellen?" Clara asked.

"No, ma'am." The lie came easily.

Later that week, Clara sent me into Dick's workroom to pack his wooden manikins into cardboard boxes. Each doll had to be carefully covered with newspaper and lowered gently into a box, much as we had lowered Dick into the grave. It was September, and the last of the sun lay on the floor of the dusty loft. It shone on the miniature town of little people standing silent, as if mindful of Dick's demise. A radiant Ellen doll smiled from atop the workbench.

I got down on one knee and lowered a jolly little fisherman, three feet high, into his cardboard box. Clerks and clergy, children, women, and cows soon followed. I was Mr. Mullins burying a happy town, a better time, a lost summer, the last of Dick White.

An hour or two later, the sun had set and the land was dark. I was almost through the packing when the main door opened below, and I heard Joe. Soon, the loft door swung open, light tumbled in, and Joe stood there looking at Dick's dolls.

"Anyone in there?"

I froze on my knees with the dolls, still and silent on the floor as Joe peered in. I stared ahead blankly with the dozen or so wooden figures still on the floor. I had joined their little village, and Joe looked but did not see me. He walked in and saw Ellen on the workbench. His pants leg brushed against my shoulder as he touched her wooden form. Eyes wide, like the others, I looked straight ahead. Soon the door swung to, and he was gone down the steps to his room. I stayed frozen like that for a time, not wanting to leave their smiling world, Eden before the snake. But soon my knees hurt, and I moved and looked around at my company. No sore knees or feet among them. No pain, no fear. Eden forever. I put them in their boxes.

The outside door opened again, and I knew it was Ellen. She went straight to Joe's little apartment. I felt my way across the workshop floor. Light was coming up through a seam between the floorboards, and I peered down through it. Directly below I saw them. Her voice raised in agitation.

As I got down closer to the hole, I smelled something familiar.

"Oh, Joe, you must believe I love you, and I need your help. Do you really want to be poor all your life? With other people looking down on you? This business is our chance for security, to be somebodies instead of nobodies."

Her arms went around his neck.

He tipped slightly back toward the door. I heard them drop onto the couch where Joe slept. They were at it for half an hour. When it was over, she got off the bed and put on her clothes without a word. She kissed Joe again as she left. I heard her go out the main door as I lay on the floor of Dick's workshop, awash in a sea of emotion.

Soon I heard Joe snoring.

The little people in the room all looked straight ahead discretely. They had heard it all many times before. As I got up, I felt something greasy on the wood where my head had rested. The tiny smear on my finger smelled pleasant, like perfume. It was Dick's Brylcreem.

# 5

# Out into the World

One night, when I was five, my mother and I had sat out on the front step. We saw a blazing light streak across the silent sky. "What's that?" I asked.

"A meteor."

"Like a comet?" My question surprised her, and she roused herself to answer me. The light of her cigarette danced between us.

"A comet has a regular orbit, like around this house."

"Like Halley's Comet?"

"It's pronounced *Haley's*, after the man who discovered it."

"Halley's," I repeated.

"A meteor has no regular orbit. It just flies wild till it crashes into something like a planet or a star."

"It dies?"

"Yes."

"I'd rather be a comet."

She sucked hard on her cigarette, which glowed like a star against the dark. Other stars loomed behind her in the velvet sky.

The 1960s were dominated by Joey Smallwood, who was still immensely popular. For example, there was a lady in Curlew named Bessy Leonard, who had been resettled from Merasheen Island with her family. There was no hospital or even a doctor on the island. She had lost her first three children in childbirth on Merasheen. The last four were born healthy in the Placentia hospital, and she was always praising Joey Smallwood. She died in Curlew in 1965 and had his picture buried in the casket with her. This was not uncommon in Newfoundland, and it is a good indication of support for any politician.

Joey was always on the television being interviewed by Don Jamieson on *News Cavalcade*, or some such program. He positively bounced with energy as he spun his answers. The agreeable Jamieson lobbed easy ones that Joey hit out of the park. He looked good to everyone except Father, who'd sit glaring at the TV muttering under his breath, "the little bastard." When the ebullient Smallwood came on the screen, Father became transfixed. A weaker man would have fled the room in the face of such discomfort, but Father stared at the premier like a stoic.

I could never understand his bitterness toward Mr. Smallwood. Perhaps Joey reminded him of some of the things he had left behind on the mainland. Joey was on TV every second day in 1965, as the Trans-Canada Highway was being built across the island. Paving machines worked full tilt as bogs were drained, hills blasted, and spruce trees bulldozed into eternity. Joey would burble to Jamieson, "We'll finish the drive in '65."

"Little bastard!"

Of course, they did *not* finish the drive in '65. The following year the paving machines were still bogged down near Come By Chance. Joey came on TV, not to explain or apologize to his thousands of admirers. No. Instead, he had a newer, bigger plan for the Happy Province. It was Come Home Year 1966.

Thousands of Newfoundlanders, or former Newfoundlanders, had gone to live on the mainland of Canada, especially in Ontario, and in the USA around New York and Boston. The plan of Come Home Year was to invite them all home for a great big party.

Ads were taken in all media in the targeted areas. The response was overwhelming. Third- and fourth-generation Canadians and Americans came looking for their Newfoundland roots. It started a decade of root-seekers. Poets and painters came home to live in coves and bays to discover the sources of their inspiration. A mini cultural renaissance occurred in Newfoundland.

Change. Change. Change. One day, Father came home and took down his sign. A week later, he got a call to go to work in Labrador City as a construction worker, and Shirley soon began substitute teaching. We came out of the wilderness. We reached the Promised Land.

I was valedictorian at our graduation ceremonies. "Teacher's pet!" Tammy Fagan snarled.

One early evening, I was sitting at the kitchen table watching Shirley smoke cigarettes. She liked to wear a sleeveless blouse and pedal-pushers right up to the cool days of fall.

The phone rang. "It's for you," she said.

"Hello."

"Hi, Felix. This is Victoria Spaulding."

"Yes, Victoria."

"Have you decided about your university?"

"Sure, I'm going to Memorial," I said.

She was now in her second year in education at Memorial University in St. John's. "Registration is Friday, and I was wondering how you were getting in to town."

"Take the bus, I guess."

"Great. Let's go in together," she said.

"Fine."

"See you Friday morning."

"Who was that?" Shirley asked.

"Victoria Spaulding. We're going in on the bus Friday to register."

"Have you decided what you'll study?"

"I don't know. Pre-law, or education, I guess."

She looked out through the kitchen window over the sink. "I got a letter from your father yesterday. He sent this for you." She reached up over the cupboard and took down a small, unopened envelope. I opened it quickly and found a handwritten note and a hundred-dollar bill. In those days, one hundred dollars was like one thousand dollars today. I laid it on the kitchen table, and Shirley's eyes opened in amazement.

The note was from Father. It read:

*You are now bound for university. This is a great step for you in the pursuit of both knowledge and of yourself. I will pay all reasonable expenses through Shirley. This one hundred dollars is for your own use. You can waste it on beer and cigarettes, or you can use it for clothes more appropriate to a university student. Or you can use it on some other, wiser expense which neither of us can yet know. I will not inquire how you spend it.*

*Your father*

When I looked up from my note, Shirley was washing the dishes. I went out and stood in the yard. The dying days of summer were in the air as August sang its last airy tunes. Overhead, a flock of sparrows winged off the stable roof in a southerly direction. The air was still warm and full of the smells of drying hay.

I went to the large gate and looked down the paved road toward St. John's and my future. The day's heat was making little waves on Joey's asphalt.

A group of kids were returning late from swimming. One was telling a story, and the others were laughing in the soft evening air. They walked, and I listened till their laughter was reduced to murmuring. I knew them all but didn't speak. The sun had set, and birdsong completed the incantation of another day.

George Williams came out of his stable and started toward his house. He saw me and changed direction in a slow arc. For the first time in years, he came through the gate between our yards. He glanced up at our house to reassure himself that Father's sign was still gone.

"Swimming will soon be over for the year," he said as the kids passed.

"Yes, sir."

"You going to university on Friday?"

"Yes. How did you know?"

"I know everything. Wisdom of the years."

"I'm taking the bus in with Victoria Spaulding," I volunteered.

"Jerome Banion going, too?"

"No. Monk was accepted at University of Toronto."

"Memorial's not good enough for him?"

I said nothing.

"You'll find it different, living in St. John's."

"How different?"

"Noisy town, full, crammed full of noisy, rude people. Cars whizzing by you from all directions. Everything paved."

He looked up at another flock of sparrows as they pitched on the stable. I knew he was thinking of his son, Jeffrey. Jeff had gone to university in St. John's the year before. At first, he had done fine, making the varsity basketball team. Then things started to go sour for him. He was dropped from the team and soon flunked out of university. The last I had heard, he was in Toronto driving a cab.

"Good luck, Felix," he said. I could tell he meant it.

"Thanks, Mr. Williams."

The next morning was Friday, and the bus arrived at 8:00 a.m. I walked out the paved road of Curlew to the main highway. It was a crisp morning, full of birdsong. The sun was tentative as a late summer's day unfurled its tent.

I saw Victoria in the distance, standing, not leaning, by the bus shelter, as though she were posing for a picture. She was pretty, and the fresh morning fitted well about her.

"Hi," I said.

"Oh, Felix!" She pretended surprise at seeing me there, like I had just dropped down from Mars. "The bus'll be along soon." As if I didn't know.

The old Fleetline bus appeared, and we were soon rumbling our way along the Conception Bay Highway to our provincial capital, St. John's.

"We were wise to sit in the front of the bus," Victoria said. "It's much bumpier in the back."

I had just followed her. She was wearing a soft white pullover and a pair of black, creased slacks. As she turned back from the window, her right leg touched mine, ever so lightly. That touch became my point of reference for the whole trip. I imagined the muscles of her firm, volleyball legs rippling around under those creases.

The bus stopped in Holyrood, where we rushed in and bought a Coke and a bag of chips. Soon, the shore of Conception Bay rolled by us and Bell Island hovered on the horizon. The cold water of the North Atlantic rolled on the beaches.

We came to the outskirts of St. John's and passed more houses than I had ever seen. The streets were all asphalt and filled with cars. A feeling of strangeness came over me, an emptiness, a fear. At the bus terminal on George Street, a damp morning fog shrouded the inner city. The pleasant excitement of Victoria's company was replaced by the excitement of St. John's. People rushed about, pushing their lives ahead of them in invisible shopping carts. So many people. Rows of tall buildings on every side of us. Buses rushing past, cars idling, the smell of gasoline fumes everywhere. Mr. Williams was right.

We took a cab to our boarding houses. Victoria dropped me at mine, and I soon found myself alone, staring at a two-storey house on the top of Aldershot Street. By now it was almost noon, and a warm sun melted through the fog enshrouding the harbour. From the hill on which my boarding house stood, I could look down at the university. I saw the trees on the western horizon. *Curlew is over those hills*, I thought.

I picked up my suitcase. It was my father's and had WALTER RYAN, CURLEW, NEWFOUNDLAND tagged to the handle. The soft, tan leather handle felt comforting as I took it firmly and made my way to the back door of my first boarding house and knocked. I heard the front door open around the other side of the house and a voice shout, "Hello? Where are you? Hello!"

I knocked again and heard the stumbling steps making their way to the back door. It was pulled open with a kick and a curse to reveal the red face of a large man who looked about seventy.

"What are you doing at the back door?"

"My name is Felix Ryan, sir, and I think this is my boarding house."

"I know that. I know that. Come in, Felix, come in."

He was wearing a white T-shirt that clung to his large belly and covered most of his belt. His jeans were faded and hung low on his hips, and he kept pulling them up as he spoke. A large comb protruded from his back pocket, and on his feet were a pair of thick woollen socks.

I had heard that in St. John's people removed their shoes when they entered a house, much like in Japan, so I removed my good pair of black leather lace-ups and left them in the back porch. The large man led me up a couple of steps to the kitchen, and then turned to face me.

"My name is Billy Crotty, and this is my house. I spoke to your mother on the phone. She seems like a fine lady."

His nose was riddled with bright red veins that continued across his cheeks. His skin was almost transparent, and his eyes were bleary and red around the lids.

He appeared to be a little unsteady on his feet and had a haste, a weariness, and an energy at the same time. He smiled a thin get-acquainted smile and turned quickly around again. "Your room is this way."

"Do I have my own room?" I ventured.

He stopped, half-turned unsteadily, and said, "Well, you have your own bed."

The house was old. It had an antebellum air of former beauty—the *bellum* being World War II. I passed a dining room with an old brass chandelier hanging from a plaster ceiling. The mouldings at the top of the walls were six inches high. The stairs were hardwood, with a worn brown carpet runner up the middle. It was anchored at the inside of every step with brass rods, and smelled of people and stains from decades ago. An elegant, curving redwood banister guided my steps to the second floor of Billy Crotty's abode.

He swung the door open somewhat grandly, and we both looked into a large room with two double beds, two dressers, and one large wardrobe, all circa Battle of the Atlantic.

"Home sweet home," Billy summed it all up with a cackle. I walked in, put my unopened suitcase on one of the beds, and followed him back to the stairs. He turned, surprised to see me following him. His neck didn't turn, but rather his whole upper body seemed to pivot from the waist. He shrugged and continued down the stairs to the kitchen. He went to the counter by the sink and took a bottle of beer, which he had evidently been drinking when I first appeared.

After a long draft from the bottle labelled DOMINION ALE, he looked at me again.

"So, you hungry or what?"

"No, thank you."

"Want a beer?"

"No, thanks."

"I have the odd beer," he said, and went to the fridge for another. "You like my house?"

"It's a very nice house, big and roomy."

"I take in two students every September for the school year." He paused for a brief recollection and took another draft from his bottle.

"Did you always live here?" I asked.

He looked hard at me, apparently unsure of how to answer, then looked away. A thick hand brushed his large red nose.

It would be fair to say he smelled funny, but it was a pleasant musty smell of beer, cigarettes, and bleach. Billy used the latter extensively in what little cleaning he did.

"I came here with Alice when we were first married. Her father died and left it to her."

He came over to the old wooden kitchen table. A calmness came over him as he slumped in his chair. He took a swig from his bottle and looked rather blankly at the far wall.

"It's nice to have a bit of company," he said at last, appearing to remember I was in the room.

"Isn't Alice here with you?"

He looked at me again, long but not hard, and his eyes went back to the wall. "No. She's gone, gone."

I did not pursue the matter.

Suddenly, he started up again. "Alice . . . Alice. . . . It's so long since I heard her name. It's years now. Nobody comes by anymore. Just the students, and they never knew her."

"When did she die?"

"Die? She's not dead. She lives on Fleming Street."

From his baggy pocket he dug out a package of Rothmans. The large fingers extracted a cigarette, which he lit with a Zippo lighter. Slumping back in his chair, he pulled an overflowing ashtray nearer to him and proceeded to fill the room with cigarette smoke.

Suddenly, the doorbell rang. Billy hid the Dominion behind a large teapot and stumbled across the floor. I heard the front door open, and the words, "Hi! I'm Gib Martin from Corner Brook!" echoed in from the street.

"Come in, come in. Glib, is it?"

"No, it's Gib. Gilbert."

"Well, come in just the same. The other fellow's already here."

The door closed, and Gib Martin stood before me. He was bigger than me, tanned and well turned out in a sports jacket and dark slacks. The front door banged again, and a pretty girl's head appeared. "Gib, honey, you forgot this." She held a little pouch or satchel, possibly toiletry articles.

Gib glided to the hall and kissed her as he retrieved the satchel. "Thanks, Marie." Then the door closed, and Gib glided back in his sharp black slacks.

"Gib Martin." A tanned hand was extended to me, the tendons and knuckles showing delicately through fine skin.

I shook it. "Felix, Felix Ryan, from Curlew."

"Where's that?"

"In Conception Bay." I thought everyone knew that.

"So, where do we sleep?"

"Felix, will you show Gib his room?" asked Billy Crotty.

"Sure. This way."

"Old house," Gib observed when we were out of earshot. "Look at this banister, and the stairs. We got a split-level back home."

"Corner Brook?"

"Mmm hmm," he agreed, looking around. He liked the room and his bed. Gib assumed the one closet and soon was filling it with his clothes and humming to himself. Sports jackets, couple of suits, dress pants, casual pants, and sweaters were all hung or stashed away. I didn't have anything to hang in a closet anyway, so I opened Father's suitcase and started putting my clothes in my dresser. Underwear and socks, shirts, and slacks were sorted by drawer, top to bottom, with pyjamas, belts, and everything else in the bottom. When I finished, Gib was lying on his bed with his hands behind his head. "So, when do we eat around here?"

"Billy just asked if I was hungry, but I said no."

"Three meals a day, Jack, that's what I signed up for. I'll forgive him for breakfast, but I got here ten to twelve, just in time for lunch."

"We call it dinner back home," I said.

"Dinner? At noon? So, what do you call dinner at six or seven p.m.?"

"That's supper, and we eat it at five thirty."

"Different!" he said, and swung his legs onto the floor. "I'm going to rustle up some chow." And he was gone, closing the door behind him with a deft flick.

I lay on my bed and intertwined my fingers behind my head. It was all strange and exciting, like finding a bird's nest in the woods, or a horse on the path by Weavers Pond. For the first time in my life, I was independent of Father, Shirley, and Curlew, and sharing a room with a new fellow who didn't know what *supper* was.

"Hamburgers!" Gib stood in the opened door. "Come on. The old guy's got hamburgers and Coke for lunch, and it doesn't look half bad." He was gone again.

The meal wasn't half bad! Gib and I and Billy Crotty sat in that old house on Aldershot Hill and ate our first meal together—burgers and Coke. Through the kitchen window we could look from the table and see Memorial University's new campus. Buildings larger than I had ever seen glinted in a peculiar pinkish brown stone. There were only six buildings and a few residences, but it was Nineveh to me, the hanging gardens of Babylon, or Cheops's great pyramid. If you had asked me that day what was the only man-made object that can be seen from space, I would have said Memorial University. I was a real North American now. Curlew was miles behind all this. 1969, come on. And the '70s, too! Let her rip!

"Another burger, Felix?" Billy asked.

"Why not," I answered royally. "Let her go for the gullies!"

"What?" Gib asked.

"Just an expression," said I. "Just a foolish expression from back home."

"Registration starts this afternoon and classes tomorrow morning," Gib said. "I'm going to do economics."

"What about you, Felix?" Billy asked.

"Education or pre-law," I said.

"Education is slack," said Gib. "Guys do education who can't get into engineering or economics."

"My mother was a teacher, and my stepmom."

"What happened to your mother?" Gib asked.

"She died when I was five. Tuberculosis, I think."

Billy asked, "What was her name?"

"Mary."

"A schoolteacher, just like Alice," he said.

"Who's Alice?" Gib asked.

"Just a friend," Billy said.

# 6

# Memorial

Memorial University was supposed to be a memorial to Newfoundland's war dead. God knows we have enough of them. But Father said it was Joey's memorial to himself.

In fairness, Joey believed in it: "Education is the answer! Education! Education will raise Newfoundland up from the mire! The mire of ignorance and defeat! No more second-class Canadians! Education!"

So Joey built his university. The largest one in Newfoundland. The only one. The little college on Parade Street had technically been a university since 1949, but it was cramped and overcrowded. To replace it, Joey had spent millions of scarce dollars to level trees and gouge out foundations on an old farm. He made millionaires of his friends and supporters in the construction trades, and put thousands of people to work. A huge celebratory opening was held. Eleanor Roosevelt presented the keys of the new institution to newspaper magnate Lord Thompson of Fleet, the new chancellor.

Joey then persuaded Lord Taylor of Harlow, a Labour Peer, to come over from England to serve as its first president. A fine house was built for him on the shore of nearby Long Pond. Everyone observed that it was good. Especially Joey. He expounded and pontificated on the magnificence and beneficence of the new university. Professors were hired from all over the world. Half the English Department was from South Africa. Chemists came from India. Then they waited for the students to appear.

But the students didn't come. Young rural Newfoundlanders were used to a life of fishing and building houses and raising families in their home communities. Illiteracy rates were high, and dropouts were rampant. Many of those who did finish school lacked the funds to come to a strange city and pay for rent, books, and tuition at a strange institution. Their only familiar institutions were the Waterford Hospital, the Sanatorium, and Her Majesty's Penitentiary. All to be avoided if possible.

Never one to falter, Joey paid them to come. He offered free tuition and a salary to any Newfoundlander who attended his university, or as some called it, Memorial University. He built residences on campus to house them. His crony John C. Doyle paid for one, which Joey named Doyle House.

So, in 1968, Gib and I stood on Elizabeth Avenue, named for our venerable queen, and looked up at the steps of the Arts and Administration Building. Three flags waved smartly over our heads as we walked toward them, past a uniformed security guard making sure no cars parked in front of Joey's monument to learning. Neil Armstrong's landing on the moon in 1969 was anticlimactic to this!

Up those four huge concrete steps we went. A silver door-bell perched on the wall, and I wondered who would appear if I pushed it. But instead, I pushed at one of the five large glass doors in the entrance . . . and it opened to me. Me! Just as much as it opened to Gib, or to any other human being in God's crea-tion. I was a university student. That's what Joey Smallwood did for me, but I knew I could never share it with Father, who would only grind his teeth and spit, "The little bastard!"

Inside the glass doors was another row of five more glass doors leading to more steps of faux marble, twenty feet wide, with two aluminum rails on each side. The rails were capped with a honey-coloured hardwood and led to a landing at the top, a large foyer of warm, golden oak. Directly before us was the huge Little Theatre, named after one of Joey's predecessors. On the right at the top of the marble-like stairs was an information window with a lady try-ing to answer everyone's questions. Off to the left and right were two huge wooden doors that led to the offices down either hall.

The place teemed with students hurrying about with regis-tration sheets and questions:

"Where's the registrar's office?"

"Got your book list?"

"Where's the bookstore?"

"You doin' chem?"

"No, you?"

"Oh, yeah, 'cause . . ."

We were all herded up the stairs, and someone with a mega-phone shouted, "Everyone doing engineering come this way!"

The future builders and designers were then led away down one of the wings to the world of engineering.

"Everyone doing economics, this way!" I caught a glimpse of Gib talking to a pretty girl and marching off with other young economists. French. Science. Soon there were very few categories left. Probably basket weaving and education. I didn't know what I was doing, but I was not attracted to any of the other faculties. A group of about fifty of us shifted around looking at our feet and waiting for insight or revelation. "Education!" the megaphone man shouted. We had waited till the last minute before jumping, like people aboard a sinking ship. "Education, this way," he shouted again. I jumped.

The second most important building on campus was the Thompson Student Centre, where we all met to eat lunch or drink coffee. Just opened by Lord Taylor that May, it housed the student union, the student newspaper known as the *Muse*, Camera MUN, and many other offices. But we participated in none of those except the Spanish Café. There you could buy a cheap lunch, soup, sandwich, or a cola.

I was sitting on the steps, just inside the door, one day with Tammy Fagan and Victoria Spaulding. Tammy was chewing gum, and Victoria was eating her lunch.

"Got this gorgeous professor for math," Tammy chewed.

"Frank Melon?" Victoria asked.

"Yeah! You got him, too?"

"He's American, from Wisconsin. Married."

"I don't want to marry him, I just want to drool," Tammy said.

"Then lose the gum. Or move away from me," Victoria said, and covered her lunch.

"You got him, Felix?" she chewed at me.

"I don't take math."

"Everyone takes math. You need it to graduate."

"No," I said, "you can do the Humanities II option and re-place math with a science. I'm doing geography instead."

"Hardly a science," Victoria observed as she wiped her lips with a little napkin.

On the wall above our heads were hundreds of flyers advertising apartments for rent, books for sale, roommates wanted, meditation groups, and so on. They were stapled or pinned to the cork bulletin boards that ran down the wall along the two levels of stairs. We sat on the stairs like pigeons on ledges as hundreds of other students went by.

"Our professor is from India," Victoria said. "First class she tells us the exam is based a hundred per cent on the text and not on her lectures. Big mistake. Hardly anyone goes to class anymore."

"Hey, Felix!" It was Gib. He had a black knapsack slung over his back and wore a smart grey and red tracksuit. He was looking at Victoria.

"Gib, this is my friend Tammy." He did not break his gaze. "And this is Victoria. Girls, meet my roommate, Gib."

"Where are you from?" he asked Victoria.

"Curlew," she said. "Do you know where that is?

"Everyone knows Curlew is in Conception Bay," said the geographically correct Gib.

"Yes, it is." She smiled.

"I'm going down to the café for coffee. Like to join me?" He was not talking to me or Fagan.

"I've got a class now, but some other time would be good."
They walked off together down the steps.

"Make ya puke!" Fagan observed.

"Different class of folks," I said.

"What class is that?"

"The *looks and confidence* class."

"Yeah," she sighed, and leaned against my arm. "Looks and
confidence. Well, Felix, at least I got one of them."

She was right, of course. Then something funny occurred to
me. "Which one you think you got, Fagan?"

She looked up at me from the stair below, suddenly serious.
"You know which one! You see how bold and forward I am. You
know which one, don't you?" Her eyes asked me to differ.

"If you got rid of that gum and dressed like Victoria, you'd
have the other one, too," I half lied. She had the slim build all the
girls wanted, and she was starting to fill out in the right places.
A nice hairdo or even a shampoo would help.

She looked off into the middle distance down over the stairs
where Gib had led Victoria. Then she drifted off without a word.

At the supper . . . er . . . dinner table that evening, Gib was
all questions. "So, who is she?"

"Who is who?" Billy asked over a baked ham with pineap-
ple slices.

"Yeah, who, Gib?" I asked.

"You know damn well who, that Victoria girl, from Curlew."

"Curlew? Where's that, Gib?" I asked.

"It's in Concep—you know! You live there!"

"So now you know where it is, too."

"What's her last name?"

"Let me think. Pass the ham."

"That's a funny last name," our host remarked.

"Some more ham . . ." I indicated.

"Oh, here." He passed the whole plate. "Her name?"

"It's a kind of sports equipment name. I can't remember exactly."

"Cooper?"

"No."

"Winnwell?"

"No."

"Tea or coffee?" Billy asked.

"No," said Gib, and then to me: "Is she dating anyone?"

"Tea for me, please," I said.

"Jeez, Felix, you live in this little dive with a hundred people. There's probably only ten family names there."

"Careful, Gib. That kind of insult can affect a guy's memory."

He laid down his fork, got up from the table, and went upstairs to his room, slamming the door.

"Boy! He's upset," said Billy as he poured my tea. Then he sat back and sipped on his Dominion.

When I eventually went upstairs, I said to Gib, "I just remembered, it's Spaulding."

"Spaulding?" Gib echoed. He sat up on the bed, all smiles.

Victoria and Gib were soon an item on campus. They came to the café together and walked the corridors to class together. He'd wait outside her class if he finished early, and vice versa if she did. They ate lunch together, usually in the café, away from us on the steps. If we joined them, we were greeted pleasantly, as you would greet people you knew from a distant country. Before long, they were holding hands.

We pigeons were sitting on the steps one day when I saw two guys stop to size up a girl. You know the way it happens—first the physical jolt as the pupils dilate and the breath is forcibly inhaled, expanding the chest, then the cheetah-like freeze and subtle nudge to his buddy, who is also in the freeze. The whole thing happens in a second, and you'll miss it if you're not watching. On this day, I looked down the steps to see who had caused the stalking freeze. I looked and I saw a girl who was vaguely familiar:

The gum was gone and the lipstick on.
The shirt was bright and the skirt was tight.

She showed a bit of leg, and the two top buttons were open on her blouse, which was more of a man's shirt. Her hair was washed and cut in a short, saucy flip around her nape. She came up the steps like it was a runway for Versace, one firm step at a time, each step making her hips sway in a fetching manner. She wasn't what you'd call a beauty; she looked more like what you'd call, well, a whore. She mounted the steps and stood over me.

"I took your advice."

"What advice? And who are you?"

"It's Fagan," someone said.

"I know that," I said. "What happened to you?"

"Buy me a coffee and I'll tell you."

I left my buddies on the step and was dragged down to the Spanish Café by a leggy, sluttish version of my old put-down queen, Tammy Fagan.

"I'm not Fagan anymore," she informed me over a black coffee.

"Who are you now?"

"I'm Tammy, just Tammy, and you created me."

I looked at the spot of lipstick on her tooth. "I certainly did not . . . create you. I just meant for you to . . ."

"That's not important. Whatever you said made me realize that with a costume change I could join the *looks and confidence* class. I'm sick of dragging my ass around here in dirty jeans and last century's hairdo. Invisible! While the likes of Victoria Spaulding have all the fun."

She had put her hand on my arm. We were sitting quite close together on the same side of the booth. Gib and Victoria came in and stood at the opposite end of the café.

"They mustn't have recognized us," I said.

"Or they just wanted to be alone."

"Isn't it sick the way they schmooze around with each other all the time?"

"I think it's sweet," she said, and squeezed my arm.

The top two buttons on her blouse were like two sideways eyes staring at me. The opening they provided suggested rather than showed, for Fagan still had some growing to do. I pulled my arm back slowly.

"What's the matter?" she asked.

"Nothing."

"Look around you, Felix. Any guy in this room would change places with you right now."

A silence pervaded our booth as we sipped our coffee.

"Hi, Felix!" It was Gib and Victoria. "Hey, Tammy! Lookin' good!" Gib gleamed two rows of pearly whites at her. Victoria did not speak to either of us as they walked out.

"See? There's a difference right there," she said. Her hand was back on my arm. "I want you and me to be . . . to be closer," she said.

"Why me, Fagan? I'm not sure I'm comfortable with this new you."

"Not Fagan. My name is Tammy. And it's *you* because. . . . Well, I can't be going around alone. It'll look like no one wants to be with me. People trust you; they want to tell you their secrets. Besides, you're not ugly, and you're smart. Smartest kid back in school, except for Monk. Right? Bound for glory!"

So I became one of Tammy's accessories. Worn, usually on her arm as part of her new allurement, until she could catch a bigger fish, and then she could toss me back into the pond.

One night, I came home and Billy had been drinking. Perhaps it was the beer, but he appeared more animated than before, and he started talking about his departed Alice.

"She and I were married for seven years. Her family never liked me. I had no education. Just back from the war, the navy. Say, you want to hear this?" He looked at me.

"Sure." I had no place to go.

He tapped the ashes into the ashtray with keen attention.

"I never spoke about this in years, and I'm telling you the whole story."

"I don't mind."

"There was a time when I talked about nothing else. Everyone I knew, when they'd come in here, I'd regale them about me and Alice. Finally they stopped coming. Sometimes I'd try to talk about other things, but Alice was the only thing on my mind."

"Why did she leave?"

"That's the question! That's the question I spent years thinking about. She never really said. In my mind, everything was all right between us. She was an educated woman, a schoolteacher.

"Still, she seemed happy here at home. She was a marvellous cook. There was just the two of us . . ." His red eyes became conspiratorial, and he leaned his large head toward me. He had a thick head of hair, reddish with grey.

"She couldn't have any children," he almost whispered. Then proceeded in his normal voice. It was a pleasant voice, somewhat deep and base, with an occasional lilt when he smiled at an irony or a fond memory. There was also an occasional break in his voice as his pipes faltered.

"Those were the happiest days of my life. She was so full of life and so pretty. I used to take her down to the American base for a dance, and I'd say to her, 'Alice, how does it feel to be the prettiest woman in the room?'

"There'd be officers there, too, with their wives, but none could compare to Alice."

"You loved her very much," I heard myself say.

This talk of love appeared to jolt Billy from his reverie. He took another slug from his Dominion bottle. "I suppose I did. Maybe I should have told her more. . . . We weren't big on affection in the Royal Navy. But I remember when I married her I told her I would never be with another woman, and I never was. I had it made. I had Alice and this big house. I was making good money at construction work."

"How long is she gone?"

"Ten years. It started when my brother came home from Toronto and moved in here with us. He had the upstairs room where you are. He was a furniture salesman with the department stores. Woolworth was opening up a big store here, and he was sure of a job. He had been with them in Toronto for years. He needed a place to live till he got straightened away here in St. John's.

"I was up and gone to work in the mornings without a worry in the world. I remember telling the boys how I had it made. I relied on that woman. I relied . . ." He turned to his Dominion.

Then the door opened, and Gib walked in.

Winter came, and the city roads filled with snow. Sidewalks were unplowed, and we usually walked to class, arriving soaked and cold. Then, deep winter struck, and the little ponds in the city froze over. My mind went back to Weavers Pond and Healeys Pond and skating on Joneys Gully. The miserable walking made me look with envy at the guys living in the residences. Built on campus, they were linked by underground tunnels to all other university buildings. The large heating pipes had to go underground, and some brilliant person suggested the diggers widen and deepen the tunnels so students could walk to class out of the weather. That person was Joey Smallwood.

Victoria and the new Tammy already lived in the girls' residence at Burke House, and I resolved to move into one of the boys' residences next year. This would be my first and last winter slogging through the slush and mush of St. John's.

One Friday night, there was a dance at the Thompson Student Centre and we all went. Gib was an hour gussying himself up and appraising himself in the large mirror on his dresser. "How's this?" he asked seriously.

"How's what?"

"How's the sweater? Too much white with the white pants?"

The only thing on him that was not white was the big capital letter *G* on the left side of his sweater. He looked like an orderly at the General Hospital.

"You look great," I said, and his pearly whites flashed happily to complete the tone.

We met Tammy and Victoria at the entrance and checked our winter jackets at the coat check near the steps where we perched each day. Tammy was wearing lots of makeup, heels, and a kind of red lace shawl around her shoulders. It had tassels on the ends and reminded me of a crocheted tablecloth I had seen at my grandmother's house. She was looking around, no doubt for a bigger fish.

Victoria wore tight black slacks and a pink mohair top with three or four little lime-green hearts on the front. Beside her, Gib, very white, was inordinately pleased with himself.

Tammy said, "Let's go in." We could hear the music blaring from speakers bigger than some houses in Curlew. We went in, and the conversation was effectively over for the rest of the night. We had heard that a group called Lukey's Boat was playing, and I had imagined they'd be a rustic band playing lots of jigs and reels, a few two-steps, and a couple of waltzes. Not!

Their lead singer was Laverne Squires, and she, like Gib, was dressed in white. She was belting out a frenzied number that jarred me to a stop. That girl had the pipes! She could hit the high notes square on the head and skim right on to the next ones. Tammy pulled me to the front of the mob of cavorters doing a dance I had never seen. She wanted to see the band, and, of course, she wanted to be seen, which was fine with me, for I wanted to see Laverne Squires.

Long dark hair parted in the middle. Black eyes that moved from the wild passions of the songs to quiet softness when she stooped to hear a request from a young admirer. Always male. Her white outfit was a one-piece jumpsuit that went from her neck to her ankles. Around her waist ran a loose gold chain with large loops. She was illuminated crazily by a kind of wandering light that changed her white outfit to fluorescence so that she glowed like a beacon of wild, musical sensuality.

At the end of a song, she bent down on one knee to hear a request, then rose and waited for the haunting introductory chords of "White Rabbit" by Jefferson Airplane.

My eyes opened wide. What was this all about? My middle ear popped and swooped to cadences and pitches I had never heard before. My bones began to move so gently to the music and Laverne's voice.

"Let's go find Gib and Victoria," Tammy said.

"No, I want to hear this song."

"They can hear that racket in Curlew," she complained, but stayed.

I had chased a few rabbits in the woods around Curlew, but nothing like this. And what was that part about a *smoking caterpillar*? Will Patey's Caterpillar tractor blew an oil seal one time and smoked quite a bit, but again, this was different. I couldn't picture Laverne on Will Patey's tractor. But I wanted to.

I tried to relate the words to eating mushrooms gathered from the woods, but the analogy could carry me only so far. I wanted to move *slow* with Laverne, or was it *low*? Either one, please. Mind and body!

This was not a foreign language to me, for the words were familiar in a way I did not yet understand. It was poetry, alive and evocative. I loved the images and symbols because it was just the way my own foolish mind worked. The song was over too soon, but requested and played again several times during the night.

"Come on." Tammy tugged at my hand.

"Okay."

Not hard to find Gib. He was in the middle of the gymnasium dancing with Victoria. His white outfit was lit up by the overhead black lights, just like Laverne's, and he was loving it. He and Victoria seemed to be getting into this new music, hopping around and pretending to ignore each other.

"Let's leave them alone," I said to Tammy. "I'll get you a Coke."

When I returned, she was crying. She couldn't hear me because of the noise. With a Coke in each hand, I touched her shoulder with the back of my fingers so she'd see me. She looked up through raccoon eyes of ruined mascara.

"What happened?" I asked.

She sobbed, but reached for a Coke. I gave her my handkerchief. She wiped her eyes into a dark smudge. She sobbed, "I was talking to this cute guy, and I thought we were having a good time, and you know what he said?"

I knew.

"No, what did he say?"

"We were just chatting, and then he said he wanted to . . ." She broke down and wobbled on one of her heels.

"That's no big deal. It's just talk. All the boys want to do that, and some are ignorant enough to say it."

She looked at me as she took a long swig on her Coke. "Do you want to, Felix?"

I took a swig on mine and said nothing. A large swath of mascara now ribboned around her eyes in a wild Laverne Squires kind of way. Her red lips were parted and panting from her sobs. She had a new vulnerability that was a far cry from the loud and vulgar Fagan of yesterday. She had come to Memorial University as a frightened stranger like me, and she had tried to adapt, to survive, and even thrive there. She had taken a great risk in her new persona and had just paid a bitter price for it. She had truly become Tammy, and I felt my heart warm toward her.

"Yes, I do," I said.

She put her Coke behind my back, and I put my Coke behind hers, and we held each other for a moment. The music blared around us as frenzied dancing couples ignored one another coolly. Not far away, Gib grooved like a white, dancing lighthouse. The bleaching lights glared, the house-high speakers blared, no doubt rattling dishes in the china cabinets of Mount Pearl, and perhaps in China itself.

Tammy was taller than me on her heels, and her ear rubbed against the top of my head. Soon our bodies were moving to the fast music, and she said, "Wish I could dance that."

"Me, too. Let's try."

"But I can't dance with these on." She pointed to her heels.

I led her to the chairs along the side of the gym. She sat, and I bent down and took off one shoe. I gave it to her, and I took off the other one. Then, I stood up and put her left shoe in one of my pants pockets and the right in the other. They bulged out, but in this light, only two people would know they were there. In fact, I could be carrying two alligators and nobody would have noticed. In St. John's, you could drop dead on the floor with a heart attack and no one would ever notice. They would step over you all night long, and the cleanup crew would call the cops the next morning. That's how I felt that night, so long ago.

She had no shoes, and I had four. I led her out onto the floor, and we did our best to dance to the music like the others. It soon became easier. But isn't that life? Ah, life!

# 7

# Country Mouse in Residence

My final term brought my averages up, and I finished my first year on the dean's List. I won a scholarship that was touted in the local paper, and everyone at home was proud. I received several letters of congratulations from family and friends, and one came on cream paper with a watermark and a printed heading: "Wayne White, General Dealer, Curlew, New-foundland."

> Your academic achievement has made everyone in Curlew proud, and it has also assured your future success both socially and finan-cially.
> Best wishes and congratulations.
> Clara White

            PS When you get your summer holidays I
    want to see you.

Clara's wishes were not to be denied, so one day in July 1969, I found myself on the steps of White's store and walking across the linoleum I had so often swept clean. There was Ellen behind the counter serving a customer. I longed to talk to her, but she said, "Clara's out in the yard, Felix," and she pointed to the back door. Sigh!

Clara was sitting in an old Adirondack chair up by the flour store.

"Felix!" She was wearing a dark blue dress down to her ankles and a brighter blue apron to show she was still at work. When she saw me, she struggled out of the chair and motioned me to follow. It was a short walk to the flour store and the timeless Coca-Cola blonde on the sign. I reached out and pushed the heavy door open, and she stepped onto the plank floor, supporting herself with a hand on the doorpost.

The flour store smelled of confined summer heat. Relics of life from the past half-century were everywhere: hemp bags of oats, cloth sacks of flour, sacks of chicken feed stacked on pallets, and rakes, prongs, and scythe handles lodged between the eves above.

"How old are you now, Felix?"

"Seventeen."

"Seventeen. And doing well at university. Working hard. Good."

"Thank you, ma'am."

She looked around. "This place was built in 1917 by a young

man named Wayne White. He wasn't much older than you, Felix, but he was such a good-looking man." She added, "Like you'll be some day."

I was thinking to myself, *Why am I here? Why waste a summer afternoon with a batty old lady from my past?*

"Your parents must be proud."

"Yes, ma'am."

"We only had one child because . . . I had medical problems." She swallowed hard.

"Wayne built this place almost by himself. We didn't always have money, you know. We got all this the hard way." She waved her arm around at the dusty beams and ancient floors.

I studied the grinning blonde on the Coca-Cola sign.

"Now I want to see Dick's dolls," she said.

"But the steps?" I pointed to the steep ascent through the top-floor hatch.

"Never mind that. You just go up ahead of me."

I did and soon saw the old grey head emerge through the hatch, her foot lifted on steps built by her husband's hand. She stood on the second floor and turned from the handrail with a few downward brushes at her apron and dress. Then a token hand gesture smoothed her hair.

She stopped at the door to Dick's workshop and said, "I've come up here before, you know."

"With Ellen?" My mind was wandering.

"No, not with Ellen! She knows nothing!" She pushed open the door with a sigh and stepped in. The dolls were just as I had left them the previous September, when I had joined their happy village for a few minutes. Some I had entombed, while others stood standing as in life.

She walked with purpose across the floor to Dick's workbench, reached down, and found a doll that had been lying out of view under it. She lifted it from the floor into her arms and began to weep.

"Did you see the face?" she asked.

"No. I never noticed it under the bench."

"Look!"

She turned the doll toward me. On it, Dick had carved his own face. Every other face in the village wore a jolly smile, but on his face the lips were turned down, the eyelids were closed, and a silver tear sat on the cheek. Clara cradled the doll in her skinny arms and moaned, "Wooo. Wooo. Wooo."

Eventually, she stopped crying and turned to me. "I want you to put him in the box now," she said.

I took the doll from her. It felt dry and light. I knelt down on the dusty floor and wrapped paper around him. Another "wooo" from Clara came softly over my shoulder. *She's crying more over Dick's doll than she cried over Dick*, I thought.

I laid Dick in a box and closed the lid.

"Do the others, too," said Clara. "And don't forget this one." She grabbed the smiling Ellen doll from the top of the workbench. "She thinks we dreamed this store into existence. She has no idea of the work and the pain. She'll never own this place!" she cried.

"Who else can you leave it to?" I asked.

"I want to leave it to you," she said.

"Me?"

"Yes, you!"

That September, I moved into Doyle House residence to avoid the winter snow and sleet.

I registered at student housing offices on the second floor of Hatcher House, the graduate students' residence. With little fanfare, a short gentleman wearing a suit and tie duly processed me. The suit had probably fit him once, but that time was lost in the past or in the repast of good eating. It fit him so snugly that even the rolls of his love handles bulged clearly through. He handed me my key and explained the rules: No x, no y, no z, none of which bothered me, for I didn't do x, y, or z.

Seeking room 407, I dragged my father's suitcase up to the fourth floor of Doyle House, straightened my clothes, and knocked on the door.

Immediately, a deep voice answered, "Come in."

I entered a dimly lit room with the curtains drawn and only a desk light on. It was pivoted around to the adjacent bed, where a person sat wearing a shirt, vest, and plaid pants. It was difficult to see much more, for the light was focused down on the bed, where he was counting what looked like money—a lot of money.

I said, "Hi, I'm Felix Ryan, and I guess we're roommates."

He had a look of being taken off-guard. He got up, switched on the light, and held on his hand.

"Hi, I'm John Malacat," he said in a slow, deep voice. The light illuminated his unusual shape. He was over six feet tall and thin with short, curly black hair that came to a point in the centre of his forehead. His ears were also pointed and close to his head, which gave him the appearance of some kind of tall woodland dryad. He moved in the same languorous way that he spoke, almost in slow motion, and smiled in an awkward way that did not seem unfriendly.

"Just countin' some coin," he explained, and returned to the bed. There was no coin there, just bills, and all small denominations. He scooped up the money, put it in a brown paper bag, and shoved it into the bottom drawer of his desk.

"Do you lock that?" I asked.

"Can't I trust you? You got the only other key." He brushed his curly hair in the mirror, making absolutely no impression on his head, and opened the door. "I'm goin' over to the cafeteria in Hatcher House for dinner. You got a meal ticket?"

"No, I pick it up on Monday."

He put his hand into his pocket and whipped out a roll of bills. "You got any money for meals?"

"Oh, yes," I said.

"Well, if you get hungry, that's where the food is." Then he closed the door and was gone.

The room was comfortable in a contemporary, minimalist way. On each side, starting from the door, was a closet with clothes bar, hangers and five drawers, a desk with a pivoting lamp and two large bookshelves, and a bed which abutted a radiator. A large window was at the far end of the room and a mirror on the back of the door. Every bit of space was utilized in a manner I liked very much. Over the closet was a space of a foot or two to throw suitcases or boxes.

I sat on my bed. It was a lot firmer than the old ones I was used to at home or at Billy Crotty's. I sat in my chair, pulled it in to the desk, and switched on my desk light. The bookshelves showed the markings of past students, like a guy named Greg with a talent for artistic design.

The desktop was a clean, tan arborite. As I ran my hand over its smooth surface, I could imagine the white pages of a book open with the pivoting light above it. Studying would be a breeze. I was good at challenges that were clearly defined, like an academic degree program. I would triumph here, I thought. I emptied my things out on the bed and tossed the empty suitcase up on top of my closet. I hung my pants and shirts on the bar and put the rest in the drawers. Lots of room.

In the top drawer of the desk I found a Gideon Bible.

I was still reading it when the door opened and John Malacat re-entered. "Hi," he said. "Reading the Bible, eh? We've got better than that." He reached into his desk drawer and handed me a copy of *Playboy*. The young lady on the cover was enjoying her cowgirl role as she sat on a fence near a haystack. A cowboy hat and white leather boots completed her attire. Her smile was as big as Texas, and so were her . . .

"You can keep that," he said. "It's an old copy. But watch out for those stains on it. Ha."

I blushed, and he burst into laughter, rolling back on his bed and slapping his thigh. "Ha, just kidding." Then his face changed to sudden seriousness. "But don't eat the cream puffs."

"What?"

"Cream puffs. In the cafeteria. We had an outbreak of salmonella food poisoning here last year. It was the cream puffs. So, if you go to dinner tonight at the cafeteria, have apple pie."

He got up, rummaging through his closet. "Got to wear something hot downtown tonight. Got to please the ladies."

"Thursday night?"

"Sure. There's downtown every night if you know where to find it. Not much action in Curlew, I guess."

"How do you know I'm from Curlew?"

"I found out about you at dinner."

"How could you do that? I just moved in an hour ago."

"You don't think I was goin' to shack up with some guy I don't know about, do you? How dumb do you think I am?"

"Is there a file kept on everyone?"

"No, nothing like that. We have some, shall I say, mutual acquaintances. You'll see."

"Where are you from?" I asked.

"Now you're catching on." He smiled. "Grand Falls."

He picked out his clothes for the evening and laid them out on his bed. Then he showered and came back to the room smelling of aftershave. He carefully put on his shirt and tie, pants and suit. He opened his bottom drawer and took out the brown paper bag, pushed in his hand, and extracted a handful of bills. He shoved them in his pants pocket and returned the bag to the drawer. He went to the mirror to study the total effect, then turned and looked at me. "How do I look?"

"Great," I said.

"I know," he said. "Don't wait up. Ha." And he was gone.

I spent the evening studying the two books I had. Soon I got into the firm bed with the tight sheets, but sleep came quickly. I didn't even hear Malacat come in, so he must have done so quietly at a late hour. A good quality in a roommate.

I woke up starving. John's long body was mostly under the covers of his bed. One arm draped out to the floor, and a big foot splayed out at the other end. His mouth was open as he snored, and he reeked of beer and cigarette smoke. I got out as quietly as he had gotten in and went looking for the cafeteria. I had scrambled eggs, bacon, toast, tea, and orange juice, paid in cash, and sat down by myself like a king in a new country. This was going to be okay, I thought. Peyton College would be my backyard for the next two or three years.

The residences were filled with kids like myself from outside the city. Most were from the larger centres like Corner Brook and Grand Falls, but some, like me, were from the outports. It wasn't long before I met other people, and the easiest to meet were the hundred or so guys in Doyle House. Soon we were up till dawn playing sergeant major, a three-handed version of hearts, much like bridge.

I still remember the night a buzz went through our corridor and we all crowded in Bill Docker's room to hear the just-released Beatles album, *Abbey Road*. The music as much as the words conspired against the adult world that had spawned us. The rude, moral, melodic sexuality of John Lennon pointed to a new way of seeing life. Ten of us jammed in a room built for two, realizing that something amazing was happening in the music and in the world. We each went back to our room with a little glow in our eye, a little awed, reflective, and not quite the same as before. It was the same awareness that I first tasted at the Lukey's Boat dance.

When you didn't want to be interrupted in your room—say you had a girl in—you locked the door. If you were afraid your roommate would intrude, you taped the inside of the knob so the button wouldn't pop when his key turned on the outside. One day, I walked into Bill Docker's room and immediately realized someone had forgotten to lock the door. The pungent smell of parsley or sage or rosemary or thyme hung in the air like a bad fart. Docker, Malacat, and one or two other fellows looked at me with slack jaws.

"Felix, shut the door, quick," said Malacat as he rushed to open the window. Docker was pushing something into a small plastic bag and putting it into his desk drawer. His roommate, Weasel, was lighting a stick of incense. "Hari Krishna!" he greeted me with an unusually wide smile.

"What's happening?" I asked, but I already knew.

Docker turned to Malacat. "Are we in shit?"

"No, Felix is cool. It's okay." He came over to the door. "This kind of stuff has to stay absolutely secret. Do you understand?"

"Sure."

"No! Absolutely! If you had been the proctor or anyone from the college office, we would all be expelled, our university days over. Understand?"

"Yes," I said, and turned to go. Then I felt pissed off about what had just happened and said, "You guys should lock your friggin' door."

Lots of people smoked up, and a few did acid and other drugs. Some of them couldn't handle the chemicals, and their academic careers drifted away from them, and sometimes their lives. I never saw marijuana cost anyone's career or life, and toward the end of my stay at MUN, most everyone was trying it.

When John and I walked through the tunnel to Hatcher House for our first meal together, it was all, "John! Hi, John! Hey, Bad Jack! Hi, John!" Every second person greeted him. He responded to some and nodded to the rest. I walked silently beside him, very impressed. Once, a guy beckoned John aside, and they huddled, heads together under the big insulated heating pipes. Then he resumed our walk as if nothing had happened.

We sat at one of the long tables and were soon joined by other fellows and a few girls from Burke and Squires House. We chatted hockey, courses, professors, and music—the Beatles, Stones, Jefferson Airplane, Fleetwood Mac. Nothing Canadian, although Tammy and I liked Gordon Lightfoot, but definitely nothing from Newfoundland.

More and more we talked about American politics. Even as children, most of us had been shocked by the assassination of JFK in 1963. The killing of his brother Bobby and the Reverend Dr. Martin Luther King in 1968 affected us at a deep, seminal level. We were moved to fight oppression and right wrongs, and we all looked around to find an oppressor near at hand. The music of the Beatles and Stones contained a moral urging we recognized as true and real in a way no church or parent could teach us. And we had found it on our own.

We read about student marches in other cities across North America and the heavy-handed attempts to control them. We needed someone to protest against, and once again Joey Smallwood helped us out.

I remember the student march on the Confederation Building, the province's seat of government, on a cold day in 1969. We were protesting an end to free tuition, and we marched in our thousands. We were loud and peaceful and carried Joey's election signs with his picture upside down, a black X drawn through the face. Joey, in the final years of his reign, looked down from his Berchtesgaden, his tenth-floor office high over St. John's, and saw his children marching in anger below. It must have hurt.

At home, Father cheered as he watched the march on *News Cavalcade*.

We were young, we were strong, we were a generation of Newfoundlanders aware of our place in a world that begged for improvements. A new morality was needed by our parents' generation, and we were the ones to provide it. We were just starting, and casting about for other institutions of power to attack. We occupied the Arts and Administration Building like students were doing all over the Western World. It was thrilling to read about the big student uprising in Paris in 1968, which, when the trades unions joined in, almost toppled the government of Charles de Gaulle. Heroes of one generation were becoming the *bêtes noires* of the next.

The floors of the Arts Building now echoed to our sneakers instead of to the soulless soles of our masters, and the walls and halls echoed to our youthful cheers and confused slogans. We ran upstairs and took over the faculty lounge. Someone broke open the food lockers and threw sandwiches to us all. It was an experience, a sacrament, sweeter than life. We were like Che Guevara run to ground in Bolivia by the CIA, and later, like Salvador Allende and the last of his loyal followers in the presidential palace, surrounded by armed American puppets. We were against evil, murderous assassins both here and everywhere.

Viva! If only we knew who they were. Until we found out, we blamed poor Joey Smallwood and ran him from power as soon as we could. I wrote poems about the whole experience, which have mercifully been lost over time.

John Malacat did not march or occupy. When I got back from the occupation flushed with zeal and glory, his great length was stretched out on his bed reading the current *Playboy*. He rested its buxom beauty on his chest and inquired, "Well, how'd it go?"

"Great!" I raved on about the occupation with sparks flying from my eyes.

"That's really great, Felix." There was a pause. "But dinner ends in fifteen minutes. You better get moving." I grabbed my meal ticket and chased the mundane demands of the flesh, forgetting my battles with slavery and oppression.

After mid-term break, Malacat came back to residence with two pairs of red Winnwell boxing gloves. He'd been an amateur boxer in school and was quite good. His reach and skill were magnified by the ring he used for sparring—the narrow space between our two beds. He allowed other guys in to see the matches and to try their luck with the gloves. He also encouraged friendly wagers, and these soon became popular with the dozen or so boys permitted to attend. He offered odds, and before long, sums of money, considerable to a student far from home, were being exchanged. Malacat, the *house*, was doing just fine.

It all ended one night in a violent splash of blood.

Malacat was often encouraged to fight, but he didn't like it because he couldn't bet on himself, and he saw it as senseless loss of revenue. He always won, and often in a frenzy of blows that left his opponent groggy on the floor or draped over the bed.

"Don't bleed on my bed," he once screamed at a luckless opponent and bounced him on the head with a red glove. He always fought like a frightened animal, even if his opponent was inferior or weaker. His long arms delivered punishing hooks, bloodying cheeks and ears. Body blows took their breath away, and when the elbows dropped to defend, a crunching right cross or overhand usually finished the event.

One Saturday night, Malacat was still hungover from Friday and not yet ready to face another evening downtown. The matches had been boring that night, and most of the boys had already left when Docker, or Weasel Wicks, said, "Hey, John, what about a match between you and Felix?"

Malacat had not been listening. "What?"

"Yeah," someone else said, "that'd be fun to see."

"No, it wouldn't. I never boxed in my life," I said.

"None of us have, except John," was the reply.

"Yeah, we all had to try it."

"Boys, give me a break, I'm not up to it tonight," Malacat said.

"You're not up to fighting Felix!" They all laughed.

"No, not up to standing up," he said.

"John, we come here night after night losing our money to you. The least you can do is offer us a fight. Show us how it's done."

Money talked to Malacat, so to my horror he got off the bed and reached for a pair of red gloves. The other pair lay on my bed. There was no way out. I knew he liked me and would not deliberately hurt me, and I also knew the fight would be brief, because I was going to take a dive.

"Put 'em on, Felix." To their surprise, I did.

John assumed the position and backed up to the window to give me lots of room. I was going to let him hit me only once, even if it were only on the gloves, and then I was going to throw myself on the floor, or perhaps on the bed.

I had seen Father practise lots of times on the big heavy bag he had set up in the stable. The crossbeams of the old building would shake when he landed hard right and left hooks with his head down. I'd sit and watch him, not really interested, although he often asked me to try. He would name the punches as he threw them: "Right cross, left cross, uppercut, roundhouse, overhand right, left hook, right hook," and so on.

"This is a jab, Felix," he once said. "Cutest punch in the book." He extended his left arm straight as a clothesline.

"Why?"

"Because it's short and sweet. Comes so quick it almost always lands. But it rarely does much damage."

"What's the good of it, then?"

"It keeps your opponent at bay. Keeps him off you, especially if you're hurt or he's big."

"Show me again," I said, and stood up by the bag.

"Just straighten out your left arm like this." He snapped out his left arm so fast and hard it looked electric. The bag sounded and shook with the sudden jolt. "The trick is to shift the impact straight from your left shoulder to his jaw. Your arm must make contact perfectly straight. It'll put most men back on their heels if you land it right."

I tried it, and he showed me how to straighten my arm properly. "The trick is surprise. If he knows it's coming, just as well not bother to throw it. So glance away from his eye, or feint with your right hand to distract him. Count one, two, three, and hit him on **one**."

"On one?" I asked.

"The fight is over by two and three."

It all came back to me as I assumed the position between the beds. Malacat looked at me, like a cat eyeing a bird, and moved toward me as if he moved on oil. I put my gloves up to my eyes like I was supposed to. Another second and he would hit me below the elbows in my solar plexus and I would lose my breath.

I moved my right glove a bit and saw his eye follow it. Then I snapped out a perfect left-arm jab, straight as a clothesline, and he walked into it with a thud.

I opened my eyes when I heard him shout, "Jeez," and saw him back up with one hand to his face. His nose was bleeding. His back bounced off the window ledge, and, when he saw the blood, he launched himself at me. I thought this a good time to revert to my original plan and threw myself on the floor as he hurtled over me. He tripped over me and went head first into the edge of the closet with a horrible crunch. He took a step back and fell to the floor.

Dead silence in the room. When we were sure he was not going to get up, we crept over to him. The gash in his forehead went clean to the white bone and hardly bled at all.

"Man, you are dead when he comes to!" said Weasel.

I was struggling to get out of the stupid gloves. "Go down and get the proctor," I said.

"No! We'll all be in deep shit if anyone finds out. John, too. He'll kill us all."

"He needs stitches. Take off his gloves and we'll just say he fell," I said.

It took eight stitches to close the gash in John's head. When he came back from the infirmary, he was alone. I stood up, not knowing what to expect. The stitches were covered with white sticking tape over his eyebrows, and his normal pallor was worse.

"Sit down," he said. "I'm not mad with you. You did the right thing." He sat down at his desk. "At least you didn't break my nose with that jab, you sneaky little shit. I got to stay pretty for the ladies." He laughed at himself, then winced in pain.

"Go get me a couple of aspirin." He cupped the side of his head in his hand, and I ran down the corridor looking for aspirin. I never saw those red gloves again.

# 8

# Tunnels

Tammy usually met me at the entrance to the main tunnel, and we'd walk to class together. It was a five- or ten-minute walk from residence to the Education Building, and I'd walk with her as far as the Arts Building.

The tunnels ran dry and warm under the snow and sleet of the world above. They were about twelve feet wide and seven feet high, which allowed two-way traffic for even the tallest among us. The bulk of traffic was usually going one way, from the residences at 8:45 in the morning and to the residences at noon and suppertime. Like the tide going in and out. Two huge hot-water heating pipes ran from the steam plant to the academic buildings along with us. They were about eighteen inches in diameter and encased in white insulating cloth, much like very long mummified snakes, one atop the other. The tunnels were not for claustrophobics, but they were very convenient for thousands of students, and they still are today.

Five-foot-high lockers ran along both sides of the main tunnel, used mainly by students who lived or boarded in the city. They stacked away wet coats and boots, lunches and books as we walked warm and dry past them to class.

Tammy always phoned me at night before she went to bed. We would be working on assignments or studying for exams in our rooms. Sometimes we worked together, especially on weekends, and alone in my room or hers, we would soon start necking. The tape would be applied to the button on the doorknob as our academic pursuits were pushed aside.

Tammy wanted us to be a couple, and I went along for the ride. I was very fond of her, but I didn't see my future as Mr. Tammy Fagan. Her nightly calls were fond and welcomed. She said sweet things to me, and I guess I did to her. We were a comfort to each other in a strange and challenging world, and a warm place to go no matter how difficult the day had been.

Some days were very difficult. I had a devil of a time with basic economics, which was one of my electives. Elasticity of supply and demand, Keynesian economic theory, charts and graphs were foreign to me, and it took a while before I could wrestle them to the ground.

One day, I ran into a first-floor bathroom at Doyle House and saw a large, familiar shape with his head in a sink. His head came up covered with soap and two fat hands. I said, "Monk?"

"The same. And do I recognize the voice of Felix Ryan?"

He wiped the soap from his face and turned to look at me. He was just the same, except a year and a half older. "What happened to U of T?" I asked.

"Got bored. A bunch of strangers. Wanted to come back with the locals."

"Glad you did," I said, mocking his cryptic style of talking.

"I transferred down this term. Grades came with me."

"How'd you do? All A's?"

"What'd ya think?" He continued to dry himself like a big maharaja. "I heard you were in Doyle House, so I figured I'd stay here, too. Better the devil you know."

"Are you doing economics?" I asked.

"Rolston's class," he nodded. "Why?"

"Oh, just wondering. Have you eaten yet?"

"No," he said.

"Good! I'll wait for you."

We went to the cafeteria breakfast and were hardly seated when he said, "So, you and Fagan are an item."

"We've been together for almost a year now."

"How's that working out?"

"Pretty good."

"Not a union I would have predicted."

"She's changed a lot in the past year."

"I've seen her." His tone was equivocal.

"What floor you on?" I asked.

"The first, of course. No need to walk up four flights of stairs."

"Of course."

"Your roommate is an interesting piece of work."

"Malacat?"

"Mr. John Malacat from Grand Falls."

"How do you know so much? You just got here."

He ignored my comment. "His father runs a tavern and strip club called, imaginatively, 'Dirty Dicks.'"

"His father's name is Dick?"

"No, the other meaning." A lock of straight blond hair fell across his glasses. "John is also the main drug dealer in the five residences. You're not involved, are you?"

"Of course not."

"Well, if his room is raided and they find anything untoward, you could be implicated."

"Implicated?"

"Sent to jail."

I was pondering this when a familiar voice behind me said, "Anyone sitting here?"

Before we could answer, Malacat and Weasel and Docker were sitting at our table. John sat across from me, with Monk at the end and between us. "Hi, guys," I said.

"Who's your new friend?" John asked as he tasted his juice.

"This is Jerome Banion. We call him Monk back home."

"From Curlew, are you?"

"Isn't everyone?" Monk answered. Most of us laughed.

"Bit late to be settling into Doyle House."

"I just transferred in from U of T."

"Oh, wow! U of T! Impressive," Malacat said.

"No, it's just big, mostly. They have a really impressive English and law faculty, but everything else is just a bigger version of here. Lots to do, of course."

"Lots to do here, if you know where to go." John winked at his pals.

"I don't mean bars," Monk said. "I mean museums, theatre, art . . ."

"I don't mean bars either. Pass the salt," John said.

We all looked down at the salt shaker between their two hands on the table. John could reach it just as easily as Monk. It was a challenge. Monk looked at the salt shaker as we all waited to see what he would do. Then he picked it up, turned around, and threw it the length of the dining hall. It bounded along in hops and rolled into the stainless steel kicker plate at the base of the serving counter. It spun round and round, then stopped.

John looked at Monk for a moment and said, "We're not going to get along, are we?"

"That's one thing we agree on," Monk said, as to a friend.

It was a quiet breakfast.

Later that week, my phone rang. "Felix, it's Monk. I'm in the infirmary."

"What?"

"Bring me my economics book, and I'll meet you in Rolston's class." His book and notes lay on my desk, where he had been helping me with my elasticities of supply and demand.

"Why are you in the infirmary?"

"Someone put a box of tacks in my bed, and when I slid my legs in, they occasioned some nasty scratches. Nothing major. Tetanus and lockjaw shots."

"Are you okay?"

"I can't run the hundred-yard dash as well as I could, but I'll be fine."

"See you in class." I hung up the phone and looked at my watch.

"Someone in the infirmary?" John asked. He lay on his bed reading *Playboy*.

"Yeah, Monk. Some prick put tacks in his bed."

"Must have made enemies already." He went back to *Playboy*.

I got up and went to class.

After, Monk and I met Tammy in the Spanish Café. He told us about his injuries.

"In the infirmary?" she asked. "You must have been scratched up pretty bad?"

"I'll be okay."

"Who would do such a thing?"

Monk and I looked at each other. No sense telling her.

"It's been happening all week."

"What has?" I asked.

"Little terrorisms, like honey poured over my doorknob, my bed *frenched*, nasty little things. My roommate has moved out."

"Not so good," said Tammy, patting his arm.

"I'm a big boy, but I am getting tired of it."

"What will you do?"

"I don't know yet, but it may be time for a counter-strike."

"I gotta go to class," Tammy said. We kissed, and off she went.

"What's going to happen, Monk?"

He shook the hair out of his eyes. "One of two things: whoever's doing it will simply get tired and give it up. After all, he's risking getting caught each time he breaks in to vandalize my room. I've got the proctor, security, and the floor prefects on the watch, so it's getting incrementally more dangerous for him."

"Or?"

"Or he will keep it up until I leave Doyle. Then he will have won back the respect of his peers. Peers, like you, who foolishly respected him to start with," he said.

"You should have passed the salt," I said.

"I did. Remember?"

To end the feud, I stole a salt shaker from the dining hall and brought it up to the room. Uncharacteristically, Malacat was at his desk working on an assignment. Usually, he had others do them for him.

"Monk sent this," I lied, and handed him the salt shaker.

He took it in his hand and looked at the little hexagon-shaped glass body with its silver metal cap. "It's only half full," he said without looking up.

"It'll have to do," I said.

"Yes," he said, "I guess it will."

He placed the salt shaker on the top of his bookshelves, like a trophy, for all to see. His dignity had been restored.

Things quieted down for a while, and I could concentrate on my courses and enjoy my relationship with Tammy. She seemed more and more in love with me. Was I in love with her? I wrote tedious love poems that lacked both skill and sincerity. During this period, I enjoyed every course I did: psychology, philosophy, sociology, anthropology, economics (thanks to Monk), and my favourite, English literature.

We were doing Shakespeare's plays. First term: comedies. Second term: tragedies. Nothing in university, and few things in life, affected me like Shakespeare. The fine quality of his thought and the beauty of his language inspired and delighted me. I worshipped at the feet of the master. English assignments were not work for me; they were explorations into just how the master did it. If I had not been studying him as a course, I would have been reading him on my own. I wanted to get closer to the fineness of his art, his skill, his mind, his soul.

Philosophy introduced me for the first time to disciplined thought. What is life? Why am I here? Questions that were entertained by men since pre-history, by the ape-man gazing up at the stars. It gave me the chance to explore the reactions and answers to those eternal questions by the greatest minds in the world. Aristotle, Plato, Descartes, and Hobbes became my heroes. My highest mark that year was ninety-six per cent in logic, the second unit of philosophy.

In psychology, I enjoyed learning about Freud's sexual theories and how he helped bring us out of the Victorian era of guilt and prudishness. Tammy and I had brought ourselves out of it without Freud, often fuelled by the music of the Beatles and, later, the Rolling Stones. The masking tape was often on the button of the doorknob at 407 Doyle House, with Malacat politely asleep in the lobby for the night.

In sociology we learned about the Yanomami of South America and how their society reflected the same basics as our own, and of every society created by mankind. I was in my element, bringing in straight A's and boring everyone to death with my thoughts, poetry, and wild metaphors. Tammy listened to me patiently. Malacat told me to pack off and said I was taking this university thing too seriously.

"It's just a ticket to free money. Wise up, Felix. It's about money. Jeez! You need someone to take you along by the hand," he said.

He was studying commerce, intending to do postgraduate work and eventually become a banker or stockbroker. "Why a banker?" I asked him.

"'Cause that's where the money is," he quoted Willie Sutton.

Monk loved Shakespeare, too.

"Soon, you'll hear he didn't even write his own plays. Don't believe it. Nothing of the sort is remotely proven, except people's inability to accept that a human being could have written anything so pure."

"Thanks, Monk." I was not even sure why I said it.

"You know, I'm worried about your relationship with John Malacat."

"Oh, no problems there. He's all right."

"No, Felix, he's not all right. He's a drug dealer who can go to jail any day if someone were inclined to make the right phone call."

"What?"

"You have nothing in common with John Malacat. He is a criminal on his way to Dorchester Penitentiary. He may get through university, but he will surely end up in jail, or worse."

"I didn't pick him. I was assigned to the same room."

"Felix, you have to take some control of your life. You can't just float on a sea of chance and take whatever comes. What comes may not be good."

"What do you think I should do?"

"You should get Malacat out of your life. I have no room-mate. You could move in here with me." I looked around his room: bare walls, no posters, empty shelves.

"Felix, have you ever wondered why John Malacat had you for a roommate? After all, you don't have a lot in common."

"No, I never have."

"He needs a roommate like you, with a spotless reputation, so no suspicion will fall on room 407, and he can carry on his illegal affairs."

"Jeez, Monk, you're saying a lot. I'm pretty happy, so why should I just up and move out of 407?"

"Felix, you're too passive! You go along with everyone and everything. You argue with no one and object to nothing. You're a creature of inertia. Your relationship with Tammy is her idea. You live with John Malacat because you were put there. You don't have one individual idea of your own. You agree with eve-ryone, Felix!"

And I had to agree with him.

One night, John returned, very drunk, from a night downtown. At first, he was not to be found. I knocked on Docker's door, but he and Weasel were into the evening's game of sergeant major in the lobby. It was after midnight when I went into the bathroom looking for Malacat.

"John," I shouted into the shower stalls. No one about. I looked under the toilet cubicles and saw a familiar set of big feet sideways on the floor. I swung open the cubicle door and found the king of the residence unconscious on the floor. To add insult to injury, his pants were still down around his ankles from when he had toppled off the throne. I leaned into the stall. "John! John! Wake up!"

I reached in and grabbed him by the shirt. "Wake up!" But clearly, it wasn't going to happen.

I pulled his pants up around his rump and fastened his belt as well as I could. Then I started pulling him out of the stall. He started to rouse and jumped in fear. "Felix, is it you?"

"Yes. Let's get back to the room."

"Oh, no, I can't walk."

"I'll drag you. Let's go." I hoisted him with one arm over my shoulder and slid him through the bathroom door and down the hall, passing the card players as we went. Docker, Weasel, and the other players barely looked up as we dragged past, like one horrible creature from 407.

I put him on his bed, my duty done. He could clean himself up tomorrow, and the hangover was his own to deal with. I picked up the phone to call Tammy.

"I heard you're moving out," he said drunkenly from his bed.

"You can't believe everything you hear," I said, and dialled Tammy's number. "Remember to shower tomorrow," I added, but he might have been asleep.

# 9

# The Return of Ellen

One day, I got a phone call from Gib Martin. "Did you hear about Billy Crotty?" he asked.

"What are you talking about?"

"He tried to off himself," Gib answered.

"You mean suicide?"

"Yes, stupid. That's what I mean. Threw himself into the harbour. He was splashing around when someone noticed him. They got him down at the hospital now."

"The harbour? They probably had to hose him down when they got him out. Think we should go visit him?"

"I don't know. Let's wait till they get him home."

So, a day or two later, when Billy Crotty was back in his home at Aldershot Street, he received a visit from two former tenants. I think it was a Thursday night that Gib and I showed up with a dozen Dominion Ale to visit our old landlord.

"Billy, how you doing?" Gib began. "Felix and I just came down to say hello."

"Come in, boys, come in. Good to have some company."

"How you doing, Billy?"

As he led us into the kitchen, he seemed even more unsteady on his feet than the last time I'd seen him.

"Oh, okay! I jumped into the harbour!"

"That's never a good sign," I said.

"No, I s'pose not, but it worked out for the best. I'm no longer in that horrible state."

"No?"

"No. Not since I let Jesus become my personal saviour."

"How did you get from the harbour to Jesus?" I asked.

"Reverend Stone from the Tabernacle Church came down to get me."

"Good of them to care," said the Gibber.

"Oh, they care, like no one else did since Alice left," said Billy.

"What's this about Alice?" Gib asked.

"She came back to me last week," Billy said.

"Last week?" I asked.

"But her name was changed," Billy said, looking out the window, confused.

"What's her new name?" I asked.

"Ellen Monteau," he said.

The floor fell away beneath my feet.

"Did you say Ellen Monteau? Where do you know her from, Billy?" I knew that she was doing some courses.

"I don't know her at all. She just turned up here one day looking for you, Felix."

"Who is Ellen Monteau?" Gib asked.

"Gib, you don't even know who Alice is yet," I snapped.

"She was an angel," Billy said. "She knocked on the back door, just like you did, Felix."

"What did you tell her?" I asked.

"Who? Oh, I was on my way to jump into the harbour, just trying to get rid of her."

"Name from your past, Felix? Care to enlighten us?" Gib asked.

"Billy, is she at MUN? Where is she?"

"She's at MUN part-time," Billy said.

"What did she say?"

"She walked in here like she owned the place. Like Alice."

"Who's Alice?"

I sat down with my Dominion between my knees.

"She went upstairs where you used to sleep, and she smelled the air. It was strange. She told me I needed professional help," he finally said.

"Sounds like she needs a bit of help herself," Gib offered.

Billy stared off through the wall for almost a minute. Then he snapped back. "Enjoy your beer, boys. It's some good to see you again."

That night in residence, the phone rang. "It's for you," Malacat said.

"Hello," I said.

"Hello, Felix. Is this you? You sound different. Where were you?" Tammy asked.

"Tammy? Oh, hi. We went to visit Billy Crotty. I'll talk to you tomorrow." I hung up without saying goodbye.

"Trouble in Paradise?" I heard Malacat's voice inquire in the dark bedroom.

That winter, sociology classes ended and anthropology began. We were all anxious to see who our new classmates would be. Tammy had tried to get into the course with me, but couldn't for scheduling reasons. I went in the door of E-2, a large amphitheatre, looked around, and saw Ellen Monteau sitting in the front row with the winter sun shining on her hair. It was a vision that carried me back to her grade eleven classroom years before, and it all swam before me again: poetry, roses, green hills, mountain peaks, starlit skies, swimming the Hellespont, conquering Everest, duels, eating pufferfish, killing and dying for love, love, love. I sat in the back of the theatre and missed every word the professor said.

That first class, we were given course outlines and sent off to the bookstore. Ellen and I met in the door.

"Oh, Felix, hi," she said.

"Hi."

"You going to the bookstore?" she asked.

"Yes."

"Well, we'll go together." She smiled.

"Fancy meeting you in anthropology," I tried to joke.

"Yes, it promises to be a very interesting course." She still spoke with formality, but the dreamy tones of Tara were gone.

"I thought you'd have finished introductory anthropology by now," I said, looking a gift horse in the mouth.

"No, it's one of my electives."

"You and Joe Gosine still running White's shop?"

"It looked that way for a while, but then Joe got deported back to Lebanon. Did you know he was here illegally? Someone reported him."

"That's too bad."

"Yes, he was a good worker."

But I remembered Joe's fingers entwined with hers in the folds of her dress and the sounds floating up through the crack in the floor of Dick's workshop.

We went down to the tunnels and followed the pipes en route to the bookstore, where we emerged through the appropriate rabbit hole.

"It will be good to have someone I know in the class. We can help each other with assignments," she said.

"Yes," I said, "that will be . . . eh . . . great."

"You won that scholarship from law school, didn't you?"

"It was just pre-law, and they awarded five."

"How modest you are. I like that. Those scholarships are hotly sought after. They indicate to the big schools who to keep an eye on. Sorts out the winners from the losers. You're on your way, Felix!"

"I'm not even sure if I want to go to law school."

"Of course you do. Many are called, but few are chosen," she quoted.

She wore one of those party dresses of the 1960s, a Peggy Lee frilly thing that exploded out over her hips from a tight waistline. On top of it she wore a tight woollen sweater that almost said, "Find me in a malt shop and make me a movie star." We found our way to the bookstore and browsed through the books.

"Wow! Thirty dollars for three paperbacks! These books are expensive," I said.

"Know what?" She was holding the Yanomami book in her hand. "If we buy just one set of books, we could share them and split the costs." She met and held my look.

"Yes," I agreed.

"Where do you live?" I asked her.

"Burke House."

"Really? I've never seen you in the dining hall."

"I just moved in. Too much rain and snow."

"Absolutely."

"I notice we use the dining hall as a study hall after eight p.m.," she said.

"Good! Let's get together there."

"We'd better exchange phone numbers so we can arrange times."

I gave her my phone number and took hers. Soon, I was skipping my way back to Doyle House with a new poem in my heart, glowing with June sunlight in January.

"What happened to you? Win the Irish Sweepstakes?" Malacat asked.

At first I wasn't going to tell him, but I did. "I bumped into a girl. What a girl!" I fell backwards onto the bed, my feet in the air.

"You already got a girl, buddy, and she just phoned you."

Cruel reality! "What did she want?"

"Wanted her little boy to call her back."

"So, how was your first class in anthropology?" Tammy asked when I phoned.

"It was all right."

"What's the professor like?"

I couldn't even remember if it was a male or a female. "He's pretty good. Seems okay so far."

"We on for lunch?" she asked.

My mind was racing. Would Ellen be there? "Sure," I said.

"Give me half an hour to put on my makeup, and I'll meet you there."

"Sure thing." I hung up.

"Danger! Danger!" Malacat said. "You're playing with fire now!"

"What are you talking about?"

"Two cats on the one string. Someone's gonna get clawed."

"Ellen and I just . . ."

"Ellen, is it? Not that blonde who just moved into Burke?"

"The same."

"Jesus, man, don't worry about a thing. She'll be snapped up by a jock before you can shake a dick at her. What makes you think she's interested in a little shit like you?"

"I've known her for years. She's from Curlew."

"Well, I have to admit, that's a pretty good *in*, if you already know her."

"She's Aphrodite, and Newfoundland is her Cyprus. She's like . . ."

"Yeah, yeah! I heard."

After lunch, I went to Monk's room. I needed advice from the hermit crab himself. He was at his desk when I opened his door.

"No more trouble from your tormentor?" I asked.

"Not a bit lately."

"You know Ellen Monteau is in Burke House?"

"No, I did not."

"She's also in my anthropology class."

"It gets curiouser and curiouser," he said.

"She's coming on to me, and I'd like to know why."

"Hmm! Well, you are no alpha male," Monk said, putting down his book.

"I know. So, why is she interested in me?"

"Not hard to figure, really."

"Let's hear it."

"She's been married, shacked up, dated, fought over, deserted by her father and her lovers. She's tired of the hassle, and she wants to settle down with a nice guy from back home. Someone her mother will be proud of. A sensible guy with a promising career."

"Am I sensible?"

"You reek of it."

"Career?"

"She sees you as a future lawyer. A meal ticket. A permit to shop forever. She gets you in the sack once, and then she tells you she's pregnant. It won't be hard to do. Look at you. You're

a quivering, palpitating, seething mass of unclaimed testoster-
one."

"But I'm claimed. There's Tammy."

"Ah, yes. Fagan. I'm afraid she will be the first casualty of
this affair."

"The first?"

"Oh, yes, there will be others. You will be one of them."

"How do you know all this?"

"It's in Ellen's family history and in her character. She's a
deceiver and a user. She's got the looks to get what she wants,
and it's not a romp with a star jock. She wants the real deal, and
she thinks you're it."

His phone rang. "Hello. Yes, we started last Wednesday
night at seven thirty. . . . The Arts Building, room A-204. Right.
See you next Wednesday." He hung up. "I've started a chess club,
and we have twenty-eight people already."

"What am I going to do?"

"Whatever you want to. The ball's in your court. You seem
pretty happy right now with your studies and with Tammy."

"Yes, I sort of am happy, but . . ."

"But what?"

"Tammy and I are going nowhere. The relationship is all
her. I'm just taking the path of least resistance."

"That's you, Felix. That's a definition of your life: a path of
least resistance."

"I want to see if Ellen's serious about this."

"I'd say she is. You said she went looking for you at Billy
Crotty's house?"

"That's right."

"She transferred into your anthropology class, and now she turns up in residence. She's deadly serious, my friend."

Back at 407 Doyle House, I wanted to talk more about all this with Malacat, but decided against it. I could trust Monk. But Malacat? Maybe not.

The phone rang. It was Ellen. "Are we going to study hall tonight?"

"I guess so," I said.

"Let's go read about those Yanomami folks and their cute little outfits."

"What outfits?"

She laughed. "Exactly! See you there at eight?"

"See you then," I said.

Thus began my relationship with the woman of my dreams. Designing she may have been, but she sure was the most breathtaking thing I had seen on this planet. Did I know she was a schemer? Did I care? Her beauty encased me like sheer winter ice on a telephone pole.

Another question in my mind was whether Ellen knew that Clara planned to leave me the business and the house. But did I care what her motives were? No!

I brushed my hair and splashed on some Old Spice. I found my nicest shirt and brushed the wrinkles out of my jeans with my hand. As I was lacing up my sneakers, the phone rang. Tammy.

"Felix, can I come over tonight?"

"No. I'm going . . . I'm playing chess with Monk."

"I didn't know you played chess."

"He's teaching me."

"Okay, see you tomorrow."

"Bye."

I was sweating and shaking. This was going to be a rough ride. I phoned Monk right away. "If Tammy phones, tell her I'm there playing chess. Say I've gone to the bathroom or something."

"Tut, tut, tut!" was all he said.

Study hall was almost vacant, except for Ellen and me. She had the books and seemed very interested in those foreign fellows and their little penis sheaths. We looked through the three books and chatted about the course. It was an excellent way to pass an evening. I was gradually getting used to her and was not so tongue-tied.

Sudden images of her kept popping into my head: Ellen dancing in that white outfit at her wedding, Ellen in black at Dick White's funeral, Ellen sitting blonde in the sun in grade eleven. Looking at her was like studying a rare orchid, or reading a poem:

A book of verse beneath the bough
A jug of wine, a loaf of bread—and thou . . .

This will all work out, I told myself.

Soon, it was ten thirty. "I have to get back now," she said, and slid back her chair. I handed her the books. "You keep them till our next class. I've had them already. We'll change at each class."

"Great idea! Walk me to the residence?" she asked.

"Sure," I agreed. This was beginning to feel like a real date.

So, my life went on like this for a time—a deception in which I tried to juggle two girls, while not knowing how to juggle even one. I used chess with Monk, outings with Malacat, and all sorts of other lame excuses to be with Ellen. It had to end badly, and it did.

Ellen and I were beginning to talk about more than the Yanomami. We were walking back from study hall one night when she asked, "Do you miss Curlew? Your family and friends there?"

"Yes, I often do. But I'm pretty happy here, and I have to complete my degree."

"Yes," she said, "me, too."

"How's your mom?" I asked.

A dark look crossed her face. "She's fine. She was sick for a while, but now she's fine."

"What kind of sick? Was it serious?"

"I'd rather not talk about it," she said.

"What made you leave Curlew?" I asked.

"Clara and I had a falling out," was all she'd say.

The phone rang. "Hello, Felix."

"Hi, Tammy. How are you?"

"You got anything on for this Saturday?"

Mind racing: "Er . . . no."

"Good. I want to visit Billy Crotty."

"But you hardly know him."

"Victoria and Gib are always talking about him, and I want us to visit him."

"Well, yes, we can do that."

"It'll give us a chance to do something together for a change. We've been drifting apart this last month or so."

"Yes, we have," I agreed.

Saturday, we met for lunch and then took a cab to Aldershot Street to visit Billy Crotty. I went to the front door and rang the bell.

"Shouldn't we go the back way?" she asked.

"No," I said, and rang the front doorbell again.

The door opened, and Billy Crotty appeared, a dazed look on his face.

"Felix, good to see you. Come in, come on in. And a real cutie you've got with you." He winked at the well-made-up Tammy. She had a skirt up to her ass and a tight sweater open down to her breastbone.

"This is my friend Tammy."

"Nice to meet you," he said.

Billy was not alone, however. The Reverend John Stone sat at the kitchen table. I had not seen him since he had miraculously walked through our front door in Curlew. With him sat a female member of his congregation. She was about sixty, and they were both dressed as if they had just come from church. She even wore white gloves, and her white hair was frozen in a large wave at the front of her head. A bit like icing on a wedding cake.

"Greetings, fellow pilgrims," Reverend Stone said, not remembering me.

"This is Felix and his friend Tammy. He used to board here."

"Hi," we both said.

"This is Reverend Stone and Mrs. Malacat from Grand Falls. She runs our church there."

"Did you say Felix? Are you Felix Ryan?" she asked.

"Yes, I am."

"Then you must know my son John."

"John Malacat!" I heard Tammy gasp.

"Yes, ma'am, he's my roommate."

"How nice," said Reverend Stone. "It is indeed a small, if merely a temporal, world."

"Amen," said Billy Crotty. "Tea, anyone?" He put on the kettle as if we were all boarders.

The reverend had been eyeing Tammy. "Come sit down, Tammy and Felix. We can continue our prayer later."

"Thank you." We sat, now a foursome, at Billy's old kitchen table. Enough for a rubber of bridge.

"I like to chat with young people," Reverend Stone explained to Mrs. Malacat. "To exchange ideas of the world, of life, and of the Spirit."

We said nothing.

"So many of today's youth are caught up in the evils of our time, the transitory pleasures of the flesh, alcohol, drugs." He was looking at Tammy, who was doing a good impersonation of the Whore of Babylon. She had crossed one long leg over the other and stuck it out from under the table. If she'd had a cigarette, she would have tried to smoke it.

"Not that *youth* is bad or evil. No, merely tempted by these illusions, the makeup, the fleshy . . . I mean the flashy clothes and bawdy behaviour."

"Billy, how's that tea coming?" Tammy shouted.

Billy bounded in with the open newspaper fluttering in his hands. "Kettle's just about boiling."

"Give me the sports, will you?"

"Sure thing, little girl." Billy laid the pages on the table before her. "Year of the Leafs?" he half teased.

"I doubt it," she said, and buried her attention in the paper. The exchange of ideas with youth had apparently ended.

Mrs. Malacat had been looking at me with an unspoken urgency. But when the reverend went upstairs to the bathroom, she said, "How's John doing at university?"

"He's doing fine. He's passing all his courses and on the way to grad school." It was true.

"He lives with his father when he's home, and I rarely see him. Give him this." She pushed a fifty-dollar bill into my hand.

"I will, but he's got lots of money, from what I see."

"Yes. His father does well in the tavern business."

I said nothing.

It was an interesting visit. Billy was staying out of the harbour and was still alive, if a bit dopey.

In the cab on the way home, Tammy wanted to talk about us. The driver was bobbing his head to music on the radio.

"What's going on, Felix?" She looked me straight in the eye. "I want to hear it from your mouth, not from other people." Her black hair was parted in the middle, and the saucy flip was gone. One side of the part fell down across a big mascaraed eye.

"Going on?" I stalled.

"Yes, between you and me."

I blurted it out: "I don't think things are going to work out between you and me." These were the first honest words I had said to her in a month. The cab headed down over Aldershot Hill.

"Not going to work out?" she repeated.

I waited.

"What do you mean, exactly?" Her eyes were filling up, but she did not cry.

"I want to see other people."

She winced and shook her head, then calmed right down. "People like Ellen Monteau?" she asked without rancour.

"How did you know about her?"

"She came over to me in the dining hall and told me."

"Ellen told you? What did she say?"

"She said you two were dating, and that the days of Felix and Tammy are over."

I said nothing.

She looked up at me. "Felix, don't you remember that night at the Thompson Centre dance? Lukey's Boat was playing. We held each other for the first time. Does that mean nothing now?"

My silence spoke volumes. It was a long cab ride to her residence. She got out, one long leg at a time. "Goodbye, Felix." She still didn't cry as she walked away.

"I guess she stuck you with the fare, buddy," the cab driver said.

"Doyle House, please," I said.

"You can never trust the hot-looking ones," he said.

# 10

# Love

My boyhood dream was coming true. I felt like a portly Venetian merchant whose ships had come in. Walking to lunch with Ellen was like walking without the need of floors. Other guys stared or glanced enviously, but soon I didn't even see them.

All was Ellen. Ellen was all.

We soon settled into a routine. It became almost normal to sit beside her as she discussed socialization pressures on the Yanomami. The only pressures I could feel were in my heart and groin. Even now, when I remember those days, she always appears as a golden glow on a dark, cloudy day. Her smile stopped traffic and sent my poor heart into flips.

We were sitting in the cafeteria one busy lunch day when a jarring voice startled me.

"Felix!" I looked up and saw Victoria Spaulding and Gib

Martin looking down at me. "I think it's terrible the way you're treating poor Tammy!" Victoria said none too quietly.

Ellen ignored her.

"What?" I almost said, "Who?"

"To break off a relationship is one thing, but what you did was shameful."

"But I . . ."

She continued, "And sneaking around behind her back for weeks before you even told her the truth! Shame on you! You give all men a bad name!"

Gib stood silently beside her.

"I *wanted* to tell her," I said.

"See this tray of lunch?" Victoria demanded. "It's for Tammy! She's been crying in her room for three days! You both fill me with contempt."

Ellen finally spoke.

"He just didn't want to be with her! Too bad!"

Victoria said, "This can't come to any good."

"What?" I asked.

"A relationship started with this kind of pain and deceit can only end in pain and deceit."

Ellen said, "You look to your own relationship."

Victoria swept from the room and left the words hanging in the air. Then people went back to their lunch, and the noises of plates, cutlery, glasses, cups, and saucers came in like a tide to redeem the situation.

"Wow, that was awkward," Ellen said, glancing to see my reaction.

"Too bad it had to happen. Any of it," I said.

That night, I sat alone in my room. I didn't know where Malacat was, and in the square outside, a cold rain was falling into a world of wet snow. I opened my window and felt the chill. Across the square I could see Burke House in the distance, where lived my former girlfriend, Tammy Fagan. But I felt little regret for my sin against her even in that chill wind. No tears came to my eyes, just a heavy sensation around my heart.

I took off my clothes and looked around for my pyjamas. I turned and saw my reflection in the mirror. I walked toward it and saw a new human being, myself. I was taller than I remembered, and my neck, shoulders, and chest had started to fill out. Once, not long ago, I had been the height of one of Dick's dolls and had lived in a world of childhood. That doll was gone, replaced by what? I had become a university student, had broken my first heart, had knocked down John Malacat, had fallen in love. This new me lived in a new world of pain inflicted and pain received. Ah, life!

I unlocked my top desk drawer and took out an envelope I had put there when I first moved into 407 Doyle House. I took out a wrinkled hundred-dollar bill, looked at it for a moment, then put it back in the envelope and sealed it with a quick lick and a press. I printed three words on the front of the envelope: MISS TAMMY FAGAN. Next day, I surreptitiously dropped it in her mailbox. Blood money.

But the golden dream continued: breakfasts together, tunnels to class, lunches together, tunnels again, and evening meals together. Ah, the evenings! Only poetry can capture it. Perhaps Hopkins:

Brute beauty and valour and act, oh, air, pride, plume, here
Buckle! AND the fire that breaks from thee then, a billion
Times told lovelier, more dangerous, O my chevalier!

Oh, me! I sighed through the livelong day and did not wake up until the following year. I was in thrall like the knight in Keats's *La Belle Dame sans Merci*.

Malacat and everyone in my life at that time appeared slightly out of focus, as if they were moving through a fog, their bodies walking in slow motion. Reality and correct speed occurred only with Ellen Monteau.

She and I soon tired of the study hall sessions and repaired to her room or mine to be together undisturbed. Library studies progressed to fleeting kisses, and kisses were soon promoted to ecstatic necking. I longed for the sexual graduation. When it came, it was a little anticlimactic, however. I had anticipated bells ringing from the seventh heaven, angels, archangels, and assorted heavenly hosts transforming 407 Doyle House into the ceiling of the Sistine Chapel. I had anticipated the "Ode to Joy," complete with cannons firing in the (my) closing movements.

It was good, as all sex is good, but there was a peremptory manner in Ellen that troubled me. She made love as if she were on her way to an appointment. There was the act, a bit of puffing and moaning, then the finish and the cleanup. But no cigarette. No glazed-eyed reflection. No smiling ecstasy.

I happily consoled myself that I was lucky to be in bed with her at all. My friends would have lined up to tell me it was more than I deserved.

One rare evening when she and I were not together, Malacat lay on his bed reading *Playboy*, and I lay on mine reading the Bible. The big overhead light was off, and we read by our desk lamps, which were pivoted around to the beds. "For where ever your treasure is, there your heart is, too," I read aloud from the Book of Matthew.

"What?"

"Oh, just this part I'm reading about a fellow who finds a treasure in a field."

"Yeah, what happened?"

"He sells everything he has to buy the field."

"Good thinking, so he can own the treasure. Read a bit of it to me. Not too long, is it?"

I read it again, finishing with, "For where ever your treasure is, there you heart is, too."

"Jeez, that's good," said Malacat. "Let me see that for a minute." He reached over.

"Let me see your *Playboy*."

"Sure. Great article on the Kennedy assassination. Oswald didn't act alone. There were three shooters."

"No!"

So we exchanged, and I lay reading *Playboy*, and Malacat read the Bible under our separate lights as the night swirled in wind eddies in the little square below.

It would be wrong to say my term marks suffered terribly, but they suffered. I got a few A's, but no continuation of my pre-law scholarship. I told Malacat I didn't mind because I was unsure about attending law school. He just shook his head.

The academic year ended after spring semester, but Ellen and I stayed for summer school. We did a few courses, but it was mainly to be together. In September 1970, I began my third year of the B.A. program.

Malacat, especially, marvelled at my good fortune with the beautiful Ellen. I earned a modicum of respect from him and his buddies when I walked into the room with "Helen of Troy," as he called her.

"It's Ellen, not Helen," I said.

"The face that sank a thousand ships," he misquoted.

"Whatever!"

She came to the room one evening when John and I were reading. She sat on my bed and kissed me. John put down his book and was about to leave us alone.

"How are you, John? Been home lately?" she asked.

He turned from the door. "No, I pretty much stick around MUN till the semester is over."

"Must be nice to own a business like your family does."

"Just Dad running the club now. He and Mom are split."

"Oh, so sorry to hear that. Divorce is horrid for everyone."

She sat in my chair, wearing sneakers, jeans, and a loose hockey sweater. But no outfit could detract from the high cheekbones and lips carved by God. Her eyes were big and round, and their green irises shone brilliantly no matter what she was wearing. John and I just looked at her for a long, silent moment.

"Felix, I'm going out for a few hours," he announced.

"See you," I said.

"Bye, John."

When the door locked, she started to talk about the Yanomami, but I got up and pressed the button on the doorknob. Then I applied the tape.

As the end of that academic year approached, Ellen decided we should get married. I wanted to wait until one of us could make some money, but I was outvoted. On Easter weekend, I borrowed a friend's car, and we went home to Curlew to tell our parents. Father was back from Saglek in Labrador. He had lately been working on Canadian Marconi Communication's towers across the north. I think it was part of NORAD's early warning system against a Russian attack. He liked the manual work and the pay, although he was getting a bit old for the real strenuous stuff, and a bit tired of it.

"So, this is the new fiancée," he says, looking at Ellen.

"You know Ellen Monteau," I said.

"I surely do. Married to poor Dick White and buried him two years ago." Father was never one to say the right thing.

"My mother still lives in Petley," Ellen said.

"Yes, how is Maud doing these days, she and . . . ?"

"Gerald. They're doing well. He works with Eastern Bakery, driving deliveries."

In truth, Gerald had lost his licence that summer for drunk driving. I'm sure Father knew this, but for once he held his tongue.

It was a Sunday, and Shirley had cooked a turkey, an American affectation we embraced in Newfoundland since the last war. Shirley still looked great. Her hair was dark and soft, but a few lines were creeping across her face, lines of worry about Father, perhaps. She was at the sink peeling vegetables. Ellen was sitting with Father and me.

"Yes, they deliver to all the stores on the Avalon," Father said. "The bread of life," he added, senselessly, looking down at his hands on the table.

"Man does not live by bread alone," I observed.

"How true it is!" Father said. "I've been reading the Bible lately."

"He has, you know," said Shirley from the sink. "He loves it." A cigarette burned on the counter beside her.

"Oh, I had to skip the Old Testament, too boring. But I liked the evangelists, and the stories of the early Church in Acts and the Epistles. Know who my favourite character is?" He looked around the kitchen for an answer.

"Jesus?" Ellen asked.

"Good guess, but no. St. Paul. There's a fellow who stirred things up. There's a fellow who challenged authority. Had his own vision clear in his head and was prepared to lay it out for people regardless of the cost."

"Same as Jesus," I said.

"But Jesus had the big payoff, the big reputation. Son of God. Started his own church. He was only at it for three years, and even then He got himself killed. It was up to Paul and the others to sail the seas and do the spadework. Get the thing started. Know what I mean?" He looked at Ellen, who didn't respond, but just glowed in some collusion with the sunlight from the kitchen window. Father looked away from her to me. "Know what I mean, Felix?"

"Yes, I think I do." The correct answer.

"Reforming the society you live in is an important part of life, Felix. We stood up to Joey Smallwood, and now my mind is turning to the churches."

At the sink, Shirley dropped a pan.

"Yes, the churches," Father continued. "An outdated crowd of hypocrites who keep us in the eighteenth century."

"Surely, Mr. Ryan, the churches do much good with their charities and overseas work," Ellen said.

"Not really, dear. They keep those people in holy servitude and offer food at a price to the starving poor. Cultural and spiritual genocide!"

I'd come home with my girlfriend to announce our marriage, and Father was trying to change the world. A big mistake to give that man a Bible. Like giving an arsonist a can of gasoline.

"But the churches run education here in Newfoundland," Ellen said.

"Child, child," Father said to her. "We have the worst education system north of the Rio Grande River. It stops at grade eleven, when every sensible system has twelve years of schooling. Many of our students can't read. When they go to the mainland, they're put back at least one grade, often two, because they are so poorly educated by the church-run school system here in

Newfoundland. They know all about religion and nothing about mathematics. They know all about the Holy Trinity, but nothing about physics."

"Turkey's almost ready," Shirley said.

"Good, I'll help," Ellen said.

"Felix, don't you see it?" He turned to me.

"Yes, I read the Bible, too." No lie there.

"We've got to take them on. Challenge them!"

"Just us?"

"No, there must be hundreds of clear-thinking people in Newfoundland who are saying the same thing." Spittle was appearing on his lip. "I bet some of them are just back from church and are saying it to themselves at their kitchen tables right now. Right?"

"Saying what?"

"Saying the whole thing is screwed up. The churches are leading us in the wrong direction. The school system is a senseless duplication of three sets of schools, board offices, personnel, and poor little Newfoundland pays for their wasteful hypocrisy. Good line! I must write that one down." He rushed off to get a pencil.

When he came back, we were all in the dining room at the table. He stood in the door holding a pencil and a Hilroy exercise book, all ready for the debate. But we had snookered him. He quickly recovered and sat, nodding toward Ellen.

"Say a nice grace for us, Ellen."

"I'm afraid I don't know one," she said.

"Felix?" I shook my head.

He looked at Shirley, then reached out and took her hand

in his right and mine in his left. "Join hands," he said to Ellen and me.

We all linked hands around the turkey. "Father in Heaven, we are here in Curlew, joined in love. We ask You to bless this meat on our table and the four people who sit here able to eat it. Through Jesus's name, amen."

We all smiled and let go hands. Shirley said, "Amen," and I saw her looking at him with fondness, like she would at a wayward child.

The meal was delicious: turkey, dressing, boiled potatoes, carrot, parsnip, turnip, cranberry sauce, and a trifle for dessert. Father even opened a bottle of cheap Niagara wine to celebrate the occasion. He filled our three glasses and lifted his water into the air. "I propose a toast," he said, and rose to his feet.

"I drink to the health and fortune of my only son, Felix, and his betrothed, Ellen. May you be happy in your marriage like Shirley and I are in ours." I looked at Shirley, as she raised her glass and drank, as did we all. What a nice feeling I had! We settled in to finish the meal with cups of tea all round, delighted that Father had neglected his new crusade. Perhaps forgotten it.

"Well, we have to go tell Ellen's mom and Gerald our big news before we head back," I said, getting up.

"Of course, sure you do. Only right and proper," he said.

Shirley came over, put her arms around me, and gave me a kiss on the cheek. She smelled lightly of tobacco. She held me a second before she let go.

Father shook my hand. "Good luck, Felix, and you always know where we are."

They both gave Ellen a hug.

She was silent in the car as we approached the back road where Maud and Gerald lived in a trailer. Parked in the driveway was Gerald's truck, and I pulled in beside it. It was three o'clock on Easter Sunday afternoon, but ours were the first tracks in the snow to the door. No one answered our brief knock, so we went in, Ellen first. The place was damp. The smell of fried fish and bacon permeated even the stink of cigarettes and stale beer. There had been little attempt to tidy up for our visit, or even pick up the beer bottles in the small living room. Maud, sitting in front of a black and white TV, waved to us grandly. "Happy Easter," she said. She was wearing a plaid housecoat over her pink pyjamas.

"Happy Easter," I replied.

"Hi, Felix! Hi, sweetheart," she said. "Want a beer?"

Ellen said, "No, thanks. We just finished dinner at the Ryans."

"That's grand, darling," she said. "Beer, Felix?"

"Sure. Why not," I said.

She reached down to the floor beside her chair and plucked out a beer from a box just out of view. She popped it with the opener in her lap and handed it to me.

"Thanks," I said, and sat on the chesterfield across from her. Ellen joined me, but she was clearly troubled.

"So, how you been, Felix?" Maud asked.

"Just fine. Working away at the courses, trying to get ahead."

"Oh, you'll get ahead. Ellen told me all about you and how smart you are. A lawyer, eh?"

"Ellen sometimes exaggerates."

Maud smiled into her beer bottle. "What a pleasant young fellow you are. Isn't he, darling?"

"Yes, Mommy, he's wonderful."

"And you've got quite a catch there, young man." She pointed her bottle at Ellen. "The most beautiful girl who ever came out of Petley, or the whole bay." She took a gulp of beer to drink to that.

"She's extraordinary," I agreed.

Maud thought about that for a minute, and then said quietly, "Oh, I was beautiful once. You ask your father. Ask Shirley."

"I certainly believe you. I've heard that myself."

"No! Who told you that?"

"I don't remember who, exactly." I saw she was waiting eagerly, so I continued "I think it was . . . Mr. Williams."

"George Williams, from Curlew?" She smiled broadly now. "Well, that's so nice. So very nice. He remembers me, eh?"

"Yes, I heard him mention it to someone at White's shop. Is it still open?" I asked, to change the subject.

"White's shop? That old witch, Clara, is still alive, after all that's happened. She runs it with a hired girl from town, Drusilla something or other." She switched gears. "How long you two been dating?"

"It's over a year now," I said.

"Is it really that long? Seems only yesterday when she was hitched to . . ."

"Mommy, we have something to tell you," Ellen interrupted, her voice inflected with the trebles of Tara, but no Tara here.

"What is it?" Maud asked.

"Felix and I plan to be married this summer."

"This summer?" I said in surprise.

"Yes, we're in love and we'll soon be two years together."

"Well, this is really something." Maud struggled to get up. "This is really something! Gerald! Gerald, get up and come out here," she shouted toward a door that must have led into the bedroom. "This is real news."

She came toward me and encircled me with her arms, her beer bottle arched around my head, and she hugged me firmly. The same for Ellen. She pushed Ellen back at arm's length and looked at her admiringly. "She's getting hitched. She's getting hitched." Then, with the moment-destroying sense of comedy that alcohol sometimes inspires, she added, "Again!" and buckled over in laughter.

Ellen's face turned red.

"Hope it works out for you, Felix, better than . . ." But she realized the fault of her joke and swung toward the bedroom. "Gerald! Get out here. She's getting hitch . . . eh . . . married. Ellen's getting married."

"Who to?" came a sleepy voice from the little bedroom.

"Young Felix Ryan!"

"Oh," was the only answer the bedroom made. No Gerald emerged to greet the happy couple.

We soon left Maud's trailer and headed back onto the highway toward St. John's. It took Ellen about ten minutes to shake it off. Then she quickly became her loving, happy self again, as if by magic. I drove the borrowed car into my future with Ellen Monteau seated beside me. I could hardly believe my good fortune.

# 11

# Getting Hitched

Ellen wanted to be a June bride. "But June is still cold in Newfoundland. The ice is off shore, and July is warmer," I said.

"A June bride sounds so wonderful." By her dreamy tone I could tell she was into a vision of magnolias and mint juleps at her reception south of the Mason-Dixon Line.

But the thing was a grand success. Went off without a hitch that June. We rented the Avalon Lounge in Petley for the reception because it was bigger than the one in Curlew. It was much like her first wedding, to Dick White. In fact, Ellen wore the very same dress. I couldn't decide who to have for my best man, until Monk insisted that I pick Malacat. Both were full of dire predictions about the match.

Malacat said, "If you had any money, I'd be sure she was out to rob you. She's a keener, and you're a dreamer. I don't know what it is yet, but there's a game going on here."

Comfort from my friends! We didn't invite Gib and Victoria, and certainly not Tammy Fagan. I thought of Billy Crotty at the last minute, but Ellen didn't seem fussy about inviting him.

"You'd have to arrange a ride for him," she said.

"He could come out with Monk or Malacat."

"He wouldn't know a soul, and he'd have a terrible time." So, I agreed.

It was much like Dick White's wedding, but without Dick. He was out in the graveyard marking the occasion on his own.

Old Clara White attended with her new girl, Drusilla, a tall, gangly wench who looked after Clara solicitously. Midway through the reception, Ellen was dancing with someone else and I was looking around for Father. I saw Drusilla walking across the floor toward me. With little or no expression she said, "Mrs. White would like to have a dance with you."

"Is she able to dance?"

"She's able." She turned and walked back to Clara.

I went over to Clara for the next slow dance. "I'm glad you're here, Mrs. White."

"I wouldn't have missed it for the world," she said.

"Would you like to have a waltz?"

"Yes." She struggled out of her chair with Drusilla's help.

It wasn't much of a dance, really. She got one arm up over my elbow and pushed her head into my chest. In this manner, we made faltering steps with no regard for the music. If I looked straight ahead, I couldn't see her, but I could see the other couples nodding and making approving clucks as they waltzed around us.

"She's no good, you know," Clara said.

"Pardon me?"

"Ellen. She's up to no good. I want you to know that."

"No good? We're married already."

"She's a viper."

I could have argued or even protested politely, but I determined to suffer out the dance and then try to forget it.

However, Clara was not finished. "I tried to tell Dick, and look what happened to him. Now I'm telling you."

I looked down into her hard, red eyes. "I can't help myself," I said. "I love her."

"Dick said that, too." The dance mercifully ended, and I brought her back to her seat. "Thank you for the dance and the advice," I said.

"You don't believe me." She shook her head. "Just like Dick."

I headed back across the floor. I saw my Helen of Troy being returned to her table by one of the men. If she were Helen, who was I? Paris or Menelaus?

Father was wearing a tie, which I knew he hated. He was probably hoping for a fight so he could rip it off. I was watching Malacat, too, because no one liked a fight more than he did. Shirley came over and kissed me on the cheek. "Let's have a dance," she said.

"Great wedding," she said as we twirled around.

"Best one I ever had," I joked.

"Hope it'll be your last one."

"I think so."

"Ellen should make you very happy."

"How are you and Father?" I asked.

She brushed hair out of her eye. "We're fine," she said, too quickly.

"Father can be difficult," I said.

"Your father is a very unusual man."

"You know what I think, Shirley?"

"What?"

"I think everyone is unusual. Look around this room for someone normal. There's no one here from *Good Housekeeping*. We try to present ourselves that way, but really, what are we? We're all life's mutants. We're mutants from a secret planet, God knows where."

She looked at me the way I have seen her look at Father. Ever get the feeling you've said too much? To the wrong person?

After the dance, I went to the bar.

"Big day for you," my father said. We were standing at the bar, much like the one where he got the smack at Dick White's wedding. In my mind I could see Constable Higgins walking him back to our table.

"Yes, it is," I said.

"Want a drink? I've still got drink tickets left," he said.

"Sure, I'll have a beer. Cold." He had a Coke, and leaned ahead with his forearms on the bar. I did the same.

"How do you feel about it all?" he asked.

"I feel lucky."

"Yes, you are lucky to have married such a special woman. In certain Arab kingdoms, men would trade their whole flock of goats for the likes of her."

"What?"

"She would be considered such a rarity," he tried to explain.

"Goats?"

"That's the currency they deal in. But some things have no price."

"That's true," I said, and sipped on my beer as I looked around the hall. "Everyone seems to be having a good time."

"That's certainly part of it," he said.

"What's the other part?"

"You know, the usual stuff about starting a new life with the woman you love." He looked down at his Coke.

Then I realized he was not enjoying this conversation any more than I was. He was trying his best to fulfill his parental role. I was touched. I put my arm around his neck and gave him a squeeze. We were about the same height now. Short. It would take a few years, but I would bulk out in the same manner as he and eventually look quite like him. He was not a hugger, but he did not reject my embrace. I left my arm across his shoulders, and we stood there for a minute like two drunks at a bar.

I thought the wedding was a success until I got the bills from the caterers, the club, the band, and the photographers. I was flabbergasted. How were we going to pay for it?

Ellen was not worried in the least. "It'll all work out," she said. I think she meant I should work it out on my own. I did. Father came up with a thousand dollars, which saved me from borrowing it from the bank. "Pay me back when you can," he said.

Summer passed into eternity like the others.

That fall, we were living in a tidy basement apartment on Elizabeth Avenue within walking distance of MUN. Residence life was over for me because no conjugal accommodations existed. I slogged to class through a world of sleet and snow that winter. Our budget was pretty slim, but our tastes were modest. Or rather, they should have been.

"Shared difficulties can cement a relationship," I told Monk as we ate lunch together in the dining hall one day.

Monk, reading a book as he ate, mumbled something.

I continued, "We've got the furniture, kitchen gear—you know, pots and pans, cups and saucers, knives and forks, things like that."

"Got a broom and dustpan?" He *had* been listening.

"Shirley gave us a broom and dustpan."

"Then you're all set. You and the little woman."

"She's missing a lot of classes, just home cleaning and doing up the place."

"Isn't she in her final year?"

"She's supposed to graduate this spring."

"Supposed to?"

"She needs these last few credits. Four lousy months of work to complete her degree, but . . ."

"But what? Is she losing interest?"

"I can't understand her anymore. She runs around the apartment planning drapes and coordinating furniture. Now she's painting the whole thing."

"When she should be in class?"

"Exactly. Even if she doesn't want a job, at least she'd have a degree."

"What does she say?"

"Nothing. She just reads the American women's magazines and tries to transform our apartment into the White House."

I slogged home from class one day and found Ellen hanging a set of framed artistic prints on the living room wall.

"Felix, look. Aren't they precious?" She was wearing pink sweatpants and one of my white T-shirts.

"They're great! Where'd you get them?"

"Don't ask, because then you'll want to know the price, and then you'll be upset."

"Okay," I agreed. "Who wants to be upset? Not me." I went rummaging through the fridge for something to eat. "Want some Kraft Dinner and wieners?" I asked.

"Sure. Whatever you're having."

My own courses were going well. I had one more year for my first degree, a B.A. in English. Then I could apply for law school, or do a degree in education.

"You'd be silly to turn down law school," Ellen often told me.

"Why?"

"A lawyer earns ten times a teacher."

"There are unhappy lawyers, too," I said.

"Yes, but they are rich and unhappy, instead of poor and unhappy. Guess which is better."

"Shirley is a teacher, and she loves it," I said.

"Sure she does, as long as Walter is bringing in some real money."

There was a confident ring of truth in her statements.

But one day, a phone call came from home that put all our plans on hold. It was Shirley. "Felix, I'm afraid I've got some bad news. Mrs. Clara White has died."

Contrary old Clara had finally met an opponent she couldn't tell off and scare away. Cancer.

"The wake is tomorrow, and her funeral is Wednesday. Will you be in?"

"Yes, Ellen and I will be home tomorrow morning. Where's Father?"

"He's gone to the post office to mail some diatribe against the Church. Oh, Felix, he's at it again. He'll have us all excommunicated, exiled, or burned at the stake."

"Don't worry."

"Then we'll see you tomorrow."

"Who was it?" Ellen asked.

"It was Shirley. Clara White died, and the wake is tomorrow. Want to go?"

She stopped in her tracks. No answer, her eyes fixed on a wall as her mind whirled. Finally, she said, "Yes, oh yes, I want to go." She headed for her closet.

"Want some ham and eggs?" I asked.

She spent the night getting ready for her return to Curlew as Mrs. Felix Ryan. The outfit she chose was a smart-looking dark blue skirt and jacket I had not seen before. A white blouse and a small tie completed a most attractive funeral outfit. I wore my suit with a white shirt and an almost-matching tie. You only need one suit, Father used to say.

I loved Clara, and I was sad she was dead. Standing before

her coffin at the funeral home, I was amazed to see that Mullins had created a smile on her wrinkled face. A smile for whom? There was no family. Wayne and Dick were both in their graves. Drusilla sat beside the coffin, looking sad, perhaps because her job was gone to the grave with Clara. I looked at Clara's wizened old body. She'd been through it all. Kept her council and hated silently. Loved? Not that I knew about. Maybe she loved her dead husband and son? She was faithful to them, that was for sure.

"Doesn't she look lovely?" Ellen observed. *Lovely*? I thought. *She's dead!*

"Yes," I said.

"I'm really sorry, Drusilla," I said. Ellen and I shook her hand, which she offered like a cold egg sandwich.

That being done, I looked around the room for familiar faces. Father and Shirley sat away from the crowd. Across the room I saw Victoria, Gib, and Tammy, all three seated on a couch as if posing for a photograph. I saw George Williams, Doctor Phil Janes, Wilma Bartlett. The whole town was there, sitting silently around the room like Dick's village of wooden dolls. There were no tanned merchants from town at this funeral. Some of them were probably in their own private plots already, no longer on Circular Road but high on Riverside Cemetery Hill, looking down on St. John's, as they had in life.

I glanced at Tammy and saw a delicate pain in her face that caught me off guard. It was the vulnerability I had seen the night we danced in the Thompson Centre when I changed her from Fagan into Tammy.

"There's your mom and dad," Ellen said. But I didn't see hers.

"Hi," Shirley greeted us warmly. Father looked distracted, probably plotting his attack on the Church. We sat with them and settled into the occasion.

The next day was the funeral, and after a church service, we brought Clara to the graveyard and put her in the ground beside her husband and son.

They had rejoined the geology of the island they loved.

We didn't go straight back to town but went to Father and Shirley's for a meal. Amid many pleasantries, Ellen announced, "I would so love to tour the White premises."

"Why?" Father asked. "You should know the place well enough."

"It's just such an important part of our history as a town. The merchant premises. So much tradition." She dipped up a forkful of mashed potatoes and smiled at the thought.

"I don't think there'd be a problem," Shirley said.

"Who's in charge of it now? Drusilla?" I asked.

"No, I think the executor is the family lawyer, Gibbons, in St. John's," Father said.

"Let's just go over, open the gate, and walk in," Ellen suggested.

"Sure, we can do that," Father said.

So, that afternoon we parked Father's Dodge by the old shop, now closed but not yet boarded up. Father and Shirley walked up the drive from the road to the flour store. Ellen stood on the road and looked at the front facade of the shop, WHITE'S GENERAL STORE. She read the words aloud from the sign over the door.

"That sign was their statement to the world, Felix." She was looking at me with a little smile on her face.

"I want us to live here. I want that to be my sign." She pointed up at the shop.

"Why would we want to live here?"

"It'd be like going back in time. Like being able to change the past, and do it right this time."

"Change the past? Why?" I asked.

"We've both worked here, and we know how to operate a shop. I could work behind the counter, and you could deliver the groceries and do the heavy lifting. I could dress up like a modern grocer and greet my customers every morning, just like the Whites did for two generations. They were the richest family in Curlew, and everyone knew it. They were an institution, a family you could be proud of. They achieved something, Felix! They were somebodies!"

"You need to think this over, Ellen. The day of the family grocer is over. Now people go to the bigger centres like Petley or Raleigh to shop. It's less than an hour for them to drive to the new supermarkets in St. John's."

"No, Felix, the Whites made a fortune here, and people will buy most everything from us if we keep our prices competitive. We'll do things the Whites didn't think of, like a beer licence, ice cream coolers. There must be other things we haven't even considered."

"We?"

"Felix, listen to me. It's a good idea. We're so lucky you're going to inherit this place."

She knew.

"What about your degree?" I asked.

"I can finish that any time."

"What about my degree?"

"You can finish it from here and work on weekends. When you go to law school, I'll have to hire someone to help me out. Drusilla, maybe. I'm sure Mom and Gerald would help as well."

I stared at her and noticed for the first time that she was not very tall. In her sneakers, she was not as tall as me.

Father and Shirley walked back down the driveway arm in arm. "What's happening?" he asked.

"I don't know," I said.

# 12

# The Merchant Prince

I sat at my father's kitchen table with my head in my hands. "She's nuts," I said. "She's beautiful, but she's nuts."

"I agree."

"What am I going to do?"

"You can say no," he said.

"I can't say no."

"Who's in charge?" he asked.

"She is."

"No, she's not. You'll have to sign the papers."

"She'll make my life a misery unless I do. She'll sulk, pout, cry, tear out her hair, scream, accuse, threaten, and run away. She'll be at me every morning and every night."

Shirley said, "She has no money. You'll need money to stock the place and repair the outbuildings." She was standing by the fridge with her elbow resting on the top and holding a cigarette.

"You have no job, so you'll have to borrow everything. Say no! To her. It's your only chance."

"I can't."

"Then you're screwed," she said.

Father and I looked at her. We both knew she was right.

What choice did I have? I had tackled myself to my dream, and she was going to make us a merchant family from the past. At least Father and Shirley would buy groceries from us, Gerald and Maud, ourselves. Three customer families for sure. Did I know we would fail? Did I know we were doing something that would doom us? Yes and yes. But I was enthralled by my dream as much as she was enthralled by hers.

So, we were screwed, as Shirley so eloquently put it. Ellen was on a mission. She quit university and threw herself into the White premises. She bought paint and refurbished the place like *Better Homes and Gardens*. The shop and the house were hers. I was relegated to the flour store, the woodshed, the molasses store, and the coal shed to make my improvements.

My first recommendation was to tear down the coal shed, because almost no one bought coal anymore. By the early '70s, most people had electric heat or oil furnaces.

We gave our notice on the basement apartment, now tastefully appointed in contemporary American, and moved to Curlew into the White House. Father helped me with the moving, and soon we just about had the business going. The old house offered its charms, like the original cherry wood furniture from Ireland and the solid silver place settings.

But the heating was an oil stove from the '50s in the living room and a coal and wood stove to cook on in the kitchen. It was a Maid of Avalon, cast iron with some cream design work. It stood on four curved legs, had a front oven, four dampers, a top lid on one side, and a grate below the lid to poke at the embers. Above the dampers it had a large warming oven with a door hinged from the bottom. It was like going back in time, but we agreed to install electric heat as soon as we could afford it.

The plumbing was all solid, but the old water pump leaked and needed replacement. Ellen did not see this as a problem and promptly ordered a new jet pump from St. John's. The atrocious bill arrived a month later.

The bank manager came out to see the books one day and view the renovations. Ellen handled his tour, and I watched him get back into his car shaking his head.

I came from university one day in Father's truck and saw she had the old British Union Jack flying beside the new Canadian flag over the shop.

"Flags look great," I said as Drusilla served us supper.

"Next month, Felix, next month we'll be open. Look at this ad." She showed me a professional sketch for a newspaper ad announcing the grand opening of the store.

"This looks really professional," I said. The ad showed the flags and an attractive woman standing in the open door. It was Ellen herself with arms spread wide over her head. Her welcoming smile was pure Hollywood, her dress was tight, and her stiletto heels were lovely for a brothel. But for a shop?

"And that's my sign, for over the door," she said.

I would have preferred Father's sign, but I smiled. "It's certainly you."

"Phil Wallen is a professional artist from Boston. He lives in Petley, and I got him on the cheap." She smiled at her cleverness. "Phil wants to put my picture in the sign."

"Your picture up on the building, beside the words?"

"Yes, my picture and the words THE WHITE PREMISES. A visual gets more attention."

"But shouldn't we call it THE RYAN PREMISES? The Whites are in the past."

"Felix, it's easier to change the present than it is to change the past."

"What?"

We ate at the old cherry wood dining table for eight under the Waterford chandelier. Ellen usually dressed for dinner, and under Clara White's chandelier she lifted a crystal wineglass to her lips. It seemed she had finally found her dream.

"Where's Drusilla?" I asked.

"She eats in the kitchen."

"Why? Six empty places here." I pointed a silver fork.

"So she can keep an eye on the cooking."

Drusilla slipped in and out with food, as she had done for old Clara, disappearing into the dimness outside the chandelier's glow. She was lanky with a long face that showed little expression. Her clothes looked like something Clara would have worn, and may have. A dark lace shawl covered her shoulders, and she slipped it up over the back of her head like a veil, especially in the cooler months.

"Drusilla, be a dear and bring us our tea," Ellen said.

Soon, the large teapot slipped into port, like a shining silver ship from another land, perhaps China. We had taken to using cubes of sugar to utilize the little silver bowl and tongs from the cabinet. Ellen smiled at me over a steaming cup of sweet tea as she sucked on a sugar cube. Her teeth were even, but I noticed they were small and darker than the cube.

I graduated with a B.A. that spring. When I gave Ellen the news, she reached across the counter where Dick had died and took both my hands in hers. "That's so wonderful, Felix. I can't wait till you hear from law school."

"I also won a fellowship at MUN to do a master's degree in English and another in folklore."

She let go of my hands. "Folklore? Studying fairies and old songs?"

"I'm thinking about the degree in English."

"To do what? Teach English?"

"I could complete a doctorate and teach at MUN."

"A professor looks good, but they work for peanuts."

"I'm thinking about teaching high school English."

She was silent for a moment, and then said softly, "No prestige, no money. Felix, did you have any other good ideas today?"

I did not like the tone in my beloved's voice.

"I'm going over to show Father my marks." I reached down for the official transcript on the counter. Her hand shot out and covered mine.

"Felix, think. We can hang on here for three years until you get your law degree, and after that we can get out of debt."

"I'm thinking it over," I said.

The smile danced back to her face like sunbeams on a wall. "That's all I ask," she said, "and I'm sure you'll do what's best for us."

As I walked to the door, she called after me, "Felix, I love you."

One day, I followed Ellen to the clothesline. I carried the basket of wet laundry while she pinned each item to the line. The sun was shining, and a drying wind came in from the sea to touch the hayfields and clotheslines.

She worked very quickly pinning up the washing, and soon I had an empty basket. She smiled and reached her arms around my head. "Have you ever been afraid, Felix?"

I was not prepared for a question like that on so fine a day. "Of course," I said.

"Have you ever woken up in the night crying in fear?"

"No," I said.

"I have. One night I dreamed I had a sister, and we were both Untouchables in India. Do you know what Untouchables are?"

"The lowest caste."

"We slept on the sidewalk, and men kept bothering us in the night. I loved my sister, and I wanted to help her more than myself. But it was not possible. She was gorgeous, and the men kept bothering her."

"What did you do?"

"Nothing. I just woke up screaming. Mom was so mad."

"What did she say?"

"Well, she was drunk, so she was really pissed off at first. Then I told her about the dream, and she seemed to sober up."

"Did she comfort you?"

Ellen paused at the question. "In a way, she did."

"What did she say?"

Ellen looked me in the eyes for a moment, trying to decide if she would tell me. Then she shrugged and let her hands fall to her sides. "Mom said, 'Don't worry, baby, 'cause looks can get you anything.' Let's go back in, Felix. It's getting cold out here."

And she was right, the wind had turned cooler.

Father and Shirley were also delighted by my good news. Father held the transcript up to the evening light from the window and said aloud each mark in each subject. Twenty in all, five subjects a year for four years.

"Great marks! And you stuck it out for four years," he said.

"Three more for law school," Shirley burbled.

"Jeez, Felix, then you'll be a lawyer!" Father said.

"I was offered two fellowships at Memorial."

"What does that mean?" he asked.

"It means they'll pay me two thousand dollars a term to do an M.A. in English or folklore."

"Wow! They must really be impressed with you," he said.

"They offer ten or twelve each year based on marks. My English marks are my highest."

"Your logic mark is higher." He had noticed. "So, what's the most logical thing to do?" He chuckled at his own cleverness.

"Ellen wants me to push on with law school."

"Hmm," he pondered.

"What do you want?" Shirley asked.

"I don't know. I want the best for everyone," I said.

"That can be difficult sometimes," she said.

The next day was Saturday, and I had some chores in the flour store. I pushed open the red and white Coca-Cola banner that ran across the door. The pretty cola girl with the smiling red lips looked a bit like Ellen.

I poked around and eventually went up the ladder to the second floor. I pushed open the creaky door of Dick's old workshop. His vise was still attached to the workbench, and most of his tools lay about or hung on the wall. Off to the side was a pile of boxes containing most of Dick's dolls that I had packed away years before. I had been instructed by Clara to pack them for shipping, but here they were. The train had left the station without these jolly passengers. But who would want them?

Dick's perfect world of miniature Curlew folk lay waiting for their resurrection, just like himself, his father, and his mother. The early spring sun shone through the upper window and drew a perfect cross on the floor with its four small panes. The Ellen doll still stood on the workbench like a statue of the Virgin Mary.

Outside, the buds were getting fat as the sap returned to dry branches. Early birds with interesting southern experiences could be heard chirping their news in song. The frogs in Joneys Gully were feeling the warmth of the sun calling them through the mud from their boggy graves, just as God called man four and a half million years ago from the dust of the earth.

That night, I lay in bed with the one I considered the prettiest woman in creation. She turned to me and said, "So, are you going to law school?"

"Yes," I said. "If they accept my application, I'll go."

Her arms went around me, and I received the most divine gift a man could imagine. Afterwards, I lay on my back thinking. I realized I had never said no to that woman at any point in our relationship so far.

# 13

# Help from an Angel

The following month, I was accepted at Dalhousie University, to great joy at home. Ellen was so loving and affectionate that I hated to leave her for Halifax. Father loaned me his truck, and I started off on Joey's Trans-Canada Highway for the ferry in Port aux Basques that would take me to Nova Scotia. My clothes were stowed in a large cardboard box on the passenger floor. I was well stocked with a cooler full of sandwiches and bottles of Coke. There was even a cooked chicken in aluminum foil packed away, and Father had hidden a bottle of beer under it. I don't know where he got it, for there was never a beer in our house.

He walked me to the truck as Shirley and Ellen waved from the kitchen door. He took an envelope from his pocket. "I gave you a hundred dollars when you went to Memorial. Now here's another hundred to get you through Dalhousie," he said.

"Thanks, Father, but I plan to get a job in Halifax and . . ."

"There's also a letter. I don't want you to read it till you pass Deer Lake. You should get there by tonight."

"Okay," I promised.

"You never let me down yet," he said, and I thought for a minute he was going to hug me. But he just handed me the keys to the truck. "Front driver's tire has a slow leak, so keep her pumped up at the gas stations. She'll be fine for a day or two. Good luck!" Then he reached out his hand like he was signing a deal.

I happily took his honest hand in mine and gave it a shake. "I'll phone you when I get there."

"Yes, do that. Shirley and I will be waiting tomorrow night to hear from you, and I'm sure Ellen will, too."

Then Ellen ran down the path from the house in tears. Her arms were outstretched, and she threw herself around me. Father jumped out of her way. "Felix! Felix! I love you!" She smothered my face with wet kisses.

"I love you, too, Ellen," I said, holding tight to the keys. Finally, she let me go and sobbed as I started up the truck.

"Choke her," Father shouted over the din of sputtering. I realized that he meant the truck, and I pulled out the choke button. The sputtering evened out into a smooth roar. I blew the horn, waved, and pulled away from home and toward distant battles. I felt a bit like Ashley Wilkes leaving Tara for the Civil War. Scarlet waved to me sadly in the rear-view movie screen of the old Dodge.

I linked up with the Trans-Canada Highway in Holyrood, and stopped for a Coke and chips at the Fleetline Bus terminal. I had my own stash, but I just wanted to see the place again. A few people recognized me and said, "Goodbye!" and, "Good luck!" Then I jumped aboard the Dodge, popped the Coke between my legs, and gunned her out of the parking lot.

TRANS-CANADA HIGHWAY WEST, the sign said, and I sallied forth for the mainland like many others. It was a warm August day, the best time in Newfoundland, and I hated to waste it driving to Nova Scotia. I could be home puttering around the yard at some project that meant something to me. I could be in the arms of a loving and adorable wife. No, that was out. If I went back, she would be very angry with me!

I put down the window so I could hear the birds sing, but that worked only if I drove very slowly. So, I did. Eventually, I stopped the truck, got out, and sat on the tailgate. I had reached a small town called Goobies, from which a little river ran under the highway. I knew a guy in Doyle House from there. People had swum and fished in that river for a hundred years. There was an old sawmill behind the town. Suddenly, I wanted to go down and visit the mill and talk to someone. I watched some kids swim on that warm summer day, and I thought about Weavers Pond back home. Joyful birds flew over my head, and none of them were headed west like me.

Slowly, I got back into the truck and drove along toward Clarenville, listening to the birds. Faster cars passed me, and a few tooted their horns. But I drove slowly.

Around noon, I stopped at the Clarenville Irving for a bowl of pea soup. It was great. I stood in the back of the truck and looked down over Clarenville from the parking lot. It was a hearty, bustling hub town that serviced a whole region. In the distance I could see Shoal Harbour and the bridge to Random Island waving slightly in the heat and mist. Some men were fishing in the Arm.

I started up the truck and sat for a moment or two before I got on the road to Gander. There's an international airport there where Joey Smallwood ran a pig farm in the '40s. I drove past the airport exit and pushed on to Grand Falls, home of John Malacat.

I stopped at the Mount Peyton Hotel and went into the dining room. A solidly built gentleman with a thick head of black hair approached me. He was dressed in a dark suit, white shirt, and tie. "Yes, sir? Table for one?"

"Yes, please," I said, not used to that title.

He pulled out my chair with the deft move of a professional. "Menu, sir?"

It was about four o'clock in the afternoon, so why not? "Sure," I said.

He was back in a jiffy with a large pitcher of water. "Adam's Ale?" he asked.

"What?"

"Adam's Ale." He filled my glass with water. "May I recommend the special, pan-fried Atlantic salmon? It's caught locally, and it's delicious."

"Okay, I'll try it, with a cup of tea." Then, feeling a bit braver, I said, "In a teapot, not a bag in a cup."

He smiled. "A teapot is the only way we serve it, sir." He jotted down the necessary information on a small notepad, and I noticed his name tag, RYAN.

"Same name as me," I said.

"Sir?"

"I said my name is Ryan, same as yours."

"Is it, now? Where are you headed, Mr. Ryan?"

"Off to the mainland to go to university. Got all my gear out there in my father's truck."

"I've got a young fellow on the mainland playing hockey."

"Really? I don't know much about hockey."

"He's playing with the Minnesota Fighting Saints, trying to make a go of it just like you. Misses home a lot." He sighed.

"I guess I will, too."

Then another customer beckoned, and Mr. Ryan was gone.

At about six o'clock I started to think about a place to stay. The calmness of evening was settling on the land between the Springdale and Baie Verte junctions. Long shadows formed across the highway, and stands of white birch stood tall on the banks of the Indian River, where Beothuk Indians once paddled their sturdy canoes.

My mood was getting sullen as the evening thickened into night. I thought about sleeping in the truck to save thirty dollars, but the lights of the Deer Lake Motel beckoned me at about eight p.m. It was a long, one-storey building with a well-lit restaurant sporting huge glass windows. I could see families enjoying a meal. The lights were warm and inviting. It had been four hours since I ate that salmon, so I decided on a snack and a bed for the night.

The next morning, I awoke before dawn, dreaming that I was still a boy in my father's house. If I stepped out of bed in the dark, my feet would touch the cold canvas floor. Behind the wall hung my father's big sign, nailed firmly to the old wood on the front of the house.

But a new feeling was creeping through me. From the bed I looked between the motel curtains at the black sky now showing an early tinge of navy blue. A brighter blue was creeping into the fading black. A crow cawed three times. Soon, the black-blue was replaced by a grey aluminum, and the birds came out to start the day with song. I jumped out of bed onto the plaid carpet of the motel.

I thought about Mr. Ryan back at the Mount Peyton. He said his son missed home, and then I thought about Father's letter. I dug in my bag and found it crumpled under a change of clothes. The three hundred-dollar bills were nice. Then I unfolded my father's letter.

*Dear Felix:*

*So you are bound and determined to go to the mainland whence I came. Remember, when you get your degree, there is no need to live and practise there. With a wife and business here in Newfoundland, not to mention Shirley and me, you have much to come back to. I hope you will not be taken up with the charms of the mainland and forsake your home.*

He missed me! My father missed me! He was afraid I would move to Nova Scotia permanently! Ha!

It was a five-hour drive to the ferry. There was a damp mist in the air as I lugged my stuff back to the truck, and headed for Corner Brook. A copper sun burnt the mists from the lakes and rivers on my right, just as it had every August morning since the Ice Age.

Before long, I met the mountains of the west coast for the first time. But my mind went back to the low hills of home, just knolls with their heads ground down by the last glacier. We had only two landscapes at home: either the same spruce tree replicated a million times, or barren moonscapes of low hills. These were dotted with little ponds and huge grey stones called erratics, dropped there by the retreating ice.

One summer afternoon when I was four, my mother dressed me in a little coat, shorts, and hat and took me for a walk. Our gravel road led to Weavers Pond, then became a mere path into the woods. In winter, the horses and sleds dragged firewood out across the pond. I still remember the procession of horses, men, and dogs returning in the evening with loads of wood. The steam of their breath shot from the horses' noses, and the dogs yelped greetings. The men, tired and hungry, looked ahead to warm houses, families, and suppers.

But it was summer when we stopped, and Mother sat me up on a big grey rock. It was almost as high as her shoulder and flat on the top. It lay like a huge desk where some giant had been writing a book an ice age ago. She held my hand as I sat on the sun-warm rock. Robins filled the air with song, and I could smell the wild mint in the little rattling stream nearby.

"This is the Kissing Rock, Felix," she said, still holding one of my hands as I looked around.

"Kissing?" I was familiar with the word.

"When lovers were parting to go away, they would meet here and sit on this rock. If you kissed someone here, they would always come back to you."

I put my hand on her shoulder, leaned over, and kissed her cheek. She laughed gloriously, and told that story many times before she died.

But these mountains on the west coast were new, by glacial standards, with high, sharp peaks. As I crossed Birchy Narrows and headed toward Corner Brook, the road was pushed closer to the mountains by the Humber River. Just past Marble Mountain, these dark and threatening cliffs loomed over my truck like giant thugs. Frightened spruce trees clung to narrow ledges.

I looked to my right and almost put the truck off the road. The Humber River, dark, deep, secret, and sinuous, slithered along. Malacat had told me about depressed guys who just drove their cars into her and let the currents do the rest. Some of the bodies were never recovered. But the Humber River and Corner Brook did nothing to shake the new gloom stalking me. What was it?

Soon, I came to the Codroy Valley, just miles from my ferry. No surly mountains here, but soft, rolling curves and slopes with wide-open vistas as I met the Table Mountains near Port aux Basques. A bit like home, but bigger. The land began to drop away as I descended into Port aux Basques. The old Basque fishermen were long gone from these shores—slaughtered, robbed, and legislated off these grounds by the Portuguese, Spaniards, French, English, and any other gang who could get the upper hand. Off to my right I could see the Gulf of St. Lawrence, where I was bound.

I started the Dodge slowly down the winding road to the terminal. The three operative words in that sentence were *dodge*, meaning an idle walk, *slowly*, implying schoolboys moving like snails to school, and *terminal*, meaning final, like a terminal disease.

As my truck descended toward the boat, so did my heart in my chest. I began to sweat and shake a bit. I gripped the wheel with both hands and gasped for breath. Then a big old sob came out of me, and I knew I was in trouble.

I put my foot down on the brake and stopped my journey to law school. I turned into the parking lot of a small diner with a sign over the door that said LAST STOP FOR FERRY. I parked the truck where I could see it and walked in. A bunch of people were inside, probably waiting for the boat. But an eerie quiet pervaded the room, as if a robbery were in progress. People moved about and went out the door with eyes averted. Then I saw why. Over by the coolers on the other side of a pool table were two large unkempt men who appeared to be part of a motorcycle gang. Were there Hells Angels in Port aux Basques?

They finished their game of pool and stood around for a minute, exchanging a few words. Then they hugged loudly and slapped each another on their black leather backs. One of them swung around on his thick heels and swaggered out the door. I could see a fellow jumping out of his way before the door slammed shut. The other biker looked sadly at the door and sat down at the little table, now with an empty chair.

I went to the counter and ordered a big plate of french fries, gravy, and a large Coke. Out in the parking lot we could hear the departing Angel revving up his machine. The floor vibrated under my feet, and the window rattled like an Apollo moon launch. There was no place to sit, so I went over to the earthbound Angel. Any port in a storm.

"Can I sit here?" I asked.

He nodded without looking up.

So, I sat and I ate my fries. Every now and then I'd glance out the window.

"You expecting company?" he asked.

"No, just checking on my truck."

"Catching the ferry?" He placed a large steel helmet on the table beside my fries. It was a replica of the standard German army issue. I guess it was a replica. He ran his fingers through thinning hair and looked at me.

"I think so," I said.

"You think so? You don't know if you're going on the ferry?"

His honest question tapped a nerve. I looked him in the eyes and said, "When I eat these fries, and drink that Coke, I'm going to decide."

Outside we could hear the Apollo launch roaring up the hill and possibly into space.

The biker said, "I crashed my bike outside Gander. Total

writeoff. I have to get a job on the mainland, make some money, and I'll be home on a new bike by Christmas."

"Going to be cold driving a bike back home in the winter," I said.

"Yeah, and I don't want to go," he said.

"Why not?"

"'Cause I met a woman." Now he was looking me straight in the eyes.

"Who is she?"

"That guy's sister, Jasmine." He pointed at the door. We heard the last roar of the departing bike, and in the quiet of the room his words were loud. Some people had been eavesdropping, because a few murmured sadly, "Ahhhhhh," and shook their heads.

"I don't want to go either." My heart spoke the words my head did not yet know.

"Why are you going?"

"Law school at Dalhousie."

"You were accepted at Dal?"

"Yeah." I munched on my fries.

"That's a pretty good gig. I know guys who applied but never got accepted."

"They accept ten Newfoundlanders each year because we don't have a law school."

"So, what's the problem? You in love, too?"

"I don't know," I said.

"Man, you're not sure of anything!"

He reached into his pocket and pulled something out. The room went silent again, and people craned their necks to see what it was. Only a small brass case, from which he extracted a business card and handed it to me. The words YOU HAVE ASSISTED THE PEACE ANGELS were printed in raised red lettering on a white background. It reminded me of Father's sign. On top was a peace sign, and below was a cycle with angel's wings.

"If you're ever in Gander, visit our clubhouse and the boys will treat you good. Just show them that card."

"Thanks," I said, putting it in my shirt pocket.

He stood up. "Look, pal, I just decided, I'm going back to Gander. You have a safe voyage tonight." He stood in sturdy leather boots and held out his hand to me. He was tall with wide shoulders and a lanky build.

"How are you going to get there?"

"Hitchhike. I'll be there by dawn." He smiled like he was just learning how to do it.

A voice came across the quiet room. "I can take you as far as the Kippens turnoff." A bucktoothed fellow had been listening from another table. He wore a red plaid shirt and a baseball cap proclaiming some brand of beer.

"That's a good start," someone said, and other patrons nodded their approval.

"I was offered a fellowship at Memorial," I said.

Customers nodded and considered this option.

"That's great! They pay you to study, and you could stay at home," the biker said.

"Then why pay your own way to live with strangers?" the bucktoothed fellow asked.

My Coke was all gone. I reached to the round cardboard

plate and took up the last fry. I studied it for a second, then popped it into my mouth and heard myself say to the biker, "I can take you all the way to Gander."

I had put a sign up on my own house.

Sometimes there is a point in life when you are sure you made the right choice. The mind floats in a Zen-like peace, the sweet spot of existence. A rush of adrenalin surged through my veins.

The greasy-spoon customers broke into cheers and applause. Some of them followed the biker and me into the parking lot. He tossed a duffle bag into the back of the truck, and we boarded her like newlyweds embarking on life.

Bucktooth stuck his head in the driver's window and said, "You got a slack tire there on the front. Have it looked to afore you go. Garage a mile up top of the hill."

They all waved to us as we drove away, and we downed the windows and waved back. I tooted the horn. Why not? I thought. Why the hell not? I was travelling with a rough and ready biker, a lover and a renegade. For the first time in my life, I was a renegade, too. Bigger, stronger, greater! The sign was up on my house, and Father would be proud.

"My name is Bud Lambert," the biker eventually said.

"Felix Ryan." We shook hands.

"We're members of the Peace Angels. No crime, no prostitution, grand theft, auto theft, none of that. We just do good and create a peaceful environment."

"Drugs?" I asked, thinking of Malacat.

"No to that. No illegal drugs." Pause. "Except to a few close personal friends," he laughed.

So, in the company of an Angel, I headed back through the night following the signs that led me here. Now they said TRANS-CANADA HIGHWAY EAST, which would lead me home. Beside the road, the Table Mountains cavorted under dark green sheets waiting for the next glacier. The gentle Codroy River meandered through the valley, unlike the murderous Humber that lurked ahead in the woods.

Bud dozed for an hour or so, but just before Corner Brook he woke up and said, "I could sure use a beer."

"I've got one in that cooler."

"May I?"

"Be my guest."

He pulled out the chicken and placed it on the seat between us. I reached over, pulled off a leg, and munched as I drove. Bud sipped the beer, eventually realized he was hungry, too, and helped me eat the chicken. What a night! We were too excited to be sleepy, with the mountains behind us turning into deep forests outside Corner Brook. Soon we saw the lights.

"Know anybody down there?" Bud asked.

"My cousin married the guy who caught the biggest salmon in the Humber," I said.

"I don't want to go fishing," Bud said. "I want a few cold beers."

"My roommate, Malacat, has a club in Grand Falls."

"Malacat! What kind of a name is that?"

"That's his name, John Malacat."

"A club! A bridge club?"

"No, a regular club, with a bar and pool tables. You know."

"Do you want to visit your friend?"

"It's in Grand Falls," I said, thinking it over.

My evening was being filled with pivotal decisions. Twenty-four hours ago, I would not have mentioned Malacat to Bud, because I knew where the conversation would go. But this new, decisive me said, "Sure."

We passed the pushy mountains of Corner Brook. We passed the deep slithering river!

A few hours later, we took the off-ramp at Grand Falls and found our way to a sign that said DIRTY DICKS LOUNGE. We stashed our gear in the cab and locked the doors. Bud put on his Nazi war helmet and buttoned up his leather jacket.

"Do we need the helmet?" I asked.

"Badge of honour for the Peace Angels," explained Bud, an angel with no wings.

Dirty Dicks was a rundown place with a pink neon sign in the window which loudly proclaimed a name many would conceal.

"You been here before?" my new pal asked.

"No, never. You?"

He shook his head and pushed open the door.

The place was dirty and loud. It sold beer to workers from the paper mill who should have been home to their supper hours ago. A few drunken couples danced to music from a juke-box. I hesitated, but Bud walked straight to the bar and ordered two beers.

I saw a familiar form at the end of the bar.

Bud made his purchase, thanked the bartender, then turned and looked for me. "Felix, where are you?"

At my name, John Malacat looked up and saw me. In an instant, he leaped right over the bar and in two strides was upon me with a big bear hug. He lifted me off my feet. "What are you doing in Grand—"

He probably intended to say Grand Falls, but Bud, assuming that I was being attacked by a thug, smashed one of his beer bottles across the back of Malacat's head.

Malacat slumped to the floor on one knee.

I said, "Jeez, Bud! What'd you do that for? This is John Malacat."

"My God, I'm really sorry, buddy."

He and I took an arm each and pulled Malacat up from the floor and deposited him into a chair.

He soon regained his wits, and a pretty waitress held a wet towel to the back of his head. John pointed to the uniformed Nazi and said, "Who the hell is this?"

"This is Bud Lambert."

"What is he, SS?"

"No," Bud answered, "I'm a Peace Angel. We try to . . ."

"Peace Angel? You must be nuts, man. Come in here and crack me over the head with a beer bottle."

"Your organization may be misnamed, Bud," I suggested.

"I can't tell you how sorry I am. I'll make it up to you."

"How can you make it up to me? Can you treat a concussion? Can you put stitches in my head?"

John was trying to stand up, and I could tell he was about to start swinging, when Bud said, "I can work for you."

"Doing what?"

"I've been a bouncer at the Flyers Club.

"In Gander?" John sat down again.

"There's only one." Bud smiled. John smiled back. Bud held out his hand, and John shook it.

"But take off that helmet when you're in here."

Bud thought for a minute and said, "I guess I owe you that much." He took it off.

"Too bad *you* weren't wearing it, John," I said.

"Funny piece of equipment for a Peace Angel," observed Malacat. "Should be wearing a toga or beads or something like that."

"Yeah, Bud, something a bit more Gandhi," I laughed.

Bud said, "I'll bring it up at our next meeting."

"So, Felix, I guess you're on your way to law school. We heard you got accepted into Dal," Malacat said.

"Not exactly," I said. "I'm going home."

# 14

# Fall

S o, I met an angel and had an epiphany on the road to Port aux Basques. That night, we all slept at the Malacat home on Lincoln Road, and next morning, I awoke to a misty dawn and a blinding headache. I sneaked out, waking no one, and drove back to Tara.

At Mel's Mini Mart, I bought a cheap pair of sunglasses to help me face the raw morning sun which came through my windshield like an accusation. My conscience was a bit of a bother, but I was sure of my decision and ready to suffer the consequences.

Funny the way big decisions are made over a last french fry, or someone awakes in the night, turns over in the bed, and decides, *That's it! The die is cast!*

On the main drag through Gander, signs announced the Albatross Hotel, the Hotel Gander, the fast food places, and, finally, the Peace Angels' Club. But I had had enough peace for one trip, and pushed on to the Irving in Clarenville. The previous late night was catching up with me, and I felt very tired. I pulled into the parking lot in the shade of a tractor-trailer, turned off the ignition, locked the doors, and fell asleep. When I awoke, the tractor-trailer was gone and the sun was setting. I went to the Irving for supper. Then, a pot of tea restored my pristine health, and I was on the road again.

The shadows of trees lengthened as evening descended. I rolled down the window and felt the air beginning to cool and dampen. The birds were silent for another day. Moths and flying insects were about, occasionally splatting themselves onto my windshield. The tranquility of night eased my mind as the radio hummed a series of country songs, and I may even have been dozing when the moose walked out onto the road.

Two tons on the hoof and over six feet high at the shoulder, he was bigger and heavier than my truck. The mass of his belly was elevated above the bonnet to windshield height by long spindly legs. Right in line with my face!

But he stopped, big wet eyes blinded.

We came together in slow motion, and the huge head loomed across my windshield. For a fraction of a second, I thought I had missed him. I heard the thud, felt the truck shake, saw the windshield buckle in and my side mirror fly away behind me. The impact spun the truck around sideways down the road with the scream and stink of burning tires.

The engine cut out. Silence, except for a thumping sound I could not identify. It was not my breath, for I was not breathing. It was the beating of my heart! I sat in the truck listening to the thumping. The lights were still on. The front end was in a low ditch, and the back tires were still on the road. I started to breathe again, but the thumping continued. The headlights showed a myopic vision of tree branches and tall grass just over the bonnet. The windshield had one long crack running from the splintered passenger side. The convex bulge of shattered glass oozed dark blood, clotted with long brown strands of moose hair.

I gripped the wheel as a car whizzed by with glaring lights and the blare of a horn.

I got out, and my knees buckled when my feet touched the road. I hung off the door for a moment, and then stood up. I went down into the ditch to examine the damage. My side of the truck was fine. I pushed aside the branches and saw the front was fine, too, both grill and radiator intact. Wading through the tall grass, I reached the passenger side. Chunks of hide and gore were stuck in the cracked glass, and the quarter post was bent where it had struck the huge head. One long streak of blood and hair ran along the side of the truck.

My legs weakened. I got up onto the road and leaned against the tailgate. It was a clear, still night, and the stars were bright in the sky with no city lights to dull them. A hint of dampness and the tart smell of spruce were in the air.

I walked back to the moose. He was lying quietly on his side, his body and long legs down in the ditch and his head resting at road level. No breath came from the big nostrils. The sheer size of him was my first impression, his thick mass filling the ditch.

No bird, no sound, no cars. Just the moon and the stars and

me by the side of the road with a dead moose. I reached down and touched the warm thick hide. My hand rested on the coarse hair, and my mind went back to winter nights skating on Joneys Gully, when Ben Costello and I lay in the snow and looked up at the stars, trying to trace their patterns, angelic and silent. Our lives lay before us, and our choices seemed as innumerable as the stars. But this ditch held a vulgar finality that shocked me.

Then I cried. Big, gut-wrenching wails shook me as I leaned against the moose and bawled. I stayed there for a long time in the dark. A few cars went by, but no one stopped.

It was getting on toward dawn when I finally drove into the Moorland Motel parking lot, about an hour from home. The young attendant was wearing a Montreal Canadiens stocking cap, in spite of the season. He looked at the windshield.

"Jeez, buddy, what happened to you? Hit a moose?"

I nodded. "Got a water hose?"

"Out back."

"Fill her up and turn on your water pump," I said, before going into the Moorland restaurant.

I sat on a stool at the counter, and the lady said, "You could use a coffee, young fella."

Before I could ask for tea, she poured hot black coffee into my cup.

Later, behind the garage, I hosed the hair and blood off the truck. It ran red and brown down the side of the Dodge and into a sewer grate. I felt the urge to cry again but held off. The sun was up, and the truck looked almost normal. The side mirror was gone, and the windshield was shot, but it would get me home.

Soon, I was driving down Curlew's stretch of Joey's asphalt. Who would I see first? Father? Ellen? I came to the White premises and stopped. It was almost nine, so Ellen would be opening up the shop. I looked in through the front window and saw her setting up the cash register.

She looked angelic, and my heart swelled to see her. Her soft, blonde hair was upswept, with a wisp or two falling to her nape. She looked calm and self-contained as she counted the float. She wore a tidy apron over her dress and looked like a lady grocer from years past. A young Clara White, but more comely.

I pushed open the door and walked in, much like the robber who killed Dick. "Hello, Ellen."

She looked at me for the longest time without a hint of expression on her face. "Felix, I thought you were in Nova Scotia."

"I changed my mind, Ellen. I'm going to take the fellowship at Memorial."

She shut the cash drawer with a single tinny ring, then looked at me like I was a new disease. "Oh," she said. "Well, this changes *everything*." She looked back to the cash register, and her eyes glazed over, with nothing more to say to me. I went to the counter and put my two hands flat down on the wood. I faced her like Dick faced the robber. "Ellen, I don't want to be a lawyer. I want to study literature. It's what I have to do."

My words hung in the silent room for a long time before she looked up from the cash register. "Then you must do it," she said. The wooden counter stood between us. She didn't speak again, or look at me, but with one deft finger she opened the register and continued counting the money in her float.

"I'd better take back Father's truck," I eventually said.

No answer.

Father came out from the stable when he heard me pull up.

"Hello, Felix," he said, as if nothing had happened.

"I brought back your truck."

"How was Nova Scotia?"

"I didn't go. I changed my mind."

"Reconsidered, eh? Usually that's a good thing," he said, and went back into the stable. He did not even notice the mirror or the windshield.

"Felix, you're back," said Shirley, coming out into the yard. She threw her arms around my neck. "I'm so glad."

"I hit a moose outside Clarenville," I said. "Look at the windshield."

"Oh, that's nothing. Your father will get that replaced."

"I guess."

"Anything wrong?" she asked.

"I don't know," I said.

"Come in for a cup of tea?"

"No, I'd better go home." I turned and walked to the gate.

"Wait, I'll drive you."

And she did, but it did not feel like I was going home.

I was anxious about my first night back with my wife. In spite of all my attempts to explain my decision, she remained silent and introspective. I laid in bed that night, watching her in the mirror as she let down her hair. Then she got in and turned to me, waiting. She did not have to wait long, for I had missed her full body and the sweetness of kissing her. We made love with zeal. We finally broke away from each other in a sweat with half the sheets on the floor.

We lay in the dark for a time until she said, "Felix."

"Yes."

"If you had a choice between being a man or a woman, which would you choose?"

"A man, I guess. I've kind of gotten used to it."

"No, I mean sexually. Which one is better?"

"Gee, I don't know."

She rolled on her side, looked at me, and said, "Being a woman is better."

"Why?"

"Because men are always looking for it, and a woman can get it any time she wants."

Then she rolled back, and soon I heard her deep, even breathing.

I should have been sleepy and exhausted on my first night home, but I laid awake looking at the ceiling. I kept thinking back to a grave, or perhaps a ditch, where something lay dead.

Life went on much as before. That fall, I registered at MUN and started work on my first five courses in the English M.A.

program. I enjoyed the novels, poems, and more Shakespeare. I drove to town in Father's truck for my classes, and I was home most evenings for supper. If I had a night class or a major project, I stayed late to work at the library.

Ellen continued to run the shop. One night in November, I got home and she wasn't around. The house was in darkness, and the shop was locked up. I let myself in and phoned Shirley, who could not enlighten me and sounded a bit worried. Ellen had few friends she could be visiting, so where could she be?

About eleven, she came in with a sweater draped over her shoulders. "Hi, Felix, how was your day?"

"Good. My project is due Friday."

"Wow! It's cool out there." She moved closer to the stove.

"You should wear your sweater, not just lay it across your shoulders." I snuggled it around her neck. She smiled.

"Where were you?" I asked.

"Oh, just out for a walk."

"You'll soon need to wear your jacket," I said. "I'm going out for more wood."

Fall is breathtaking in Curlew. Stars wink from the sky, but when you face them, they just stare, blank and serene. Sometimes, the moon floods the ground with liquid silver. Sheds and barns glow under that silver lens. I stepped from this lunacy into the darkened woodshed and soon returned to the house with an armful of junk-length wood, my past Saturday's labour.

I looked over the far fence toward Joneys Gully, where the frogs were beginning their winter sleep and the rabbits were changing from dirty brown to purest white. An owl hooted on the hunt. A dog barked from a yard. Our kitchen window emitted a warm, yellow light that invited me in from the cold.

As I opened the back door, I thought I heard Ellen talking on the phone. I dumped the junks into the big woodbox in the porch and brought in an armful to the small box behind the stove.

"It's a splendid fall evening," I told her.

She was sitting in the rocking chair with her sweater on. "Yes," she said. "There'll be lots more of them now once Halloween is past. The next thing will be the first fall of snow."

I took the warm lifter, opened two dampers, and put a big junk into the Maid of Avalon. The wood sizzled and popped. "Let's have some tea," I said.

"That would be lovely," she said as I filled the kettle.

About two weeks after that, I worked late, and again she was not home. I was in bed when she arrived. She crawled in beside me and whispered, "Asleep?"

"No."

She put her arm under my neck, and we laid there for a time. "Want to make love?" she asked.

We did make love, and with more physical enthusiasm than ever before. I felt a nameless desperation that doubled my passion for her. The next morning, I awoke before her and laid watching her back and shoulder move with each breath. There was a faint new smell about her—a mixture of oil paint and cigarette smoke.

"I've got a job, that's all," she answered me over breakfast.

"A job doing what?"

"I model part-time for Phil Wallen in Petley."

"The artist? The one who designed our publicity photos?"

"That's right."

"How do you get home in the nights?"

"Phil drops me off." She said it casually.

"But you already have a job running the shop."

"Well, your law career is down the tubes, and we need the extra money."

"This isn't right," I said.

"What are you saying, Felix? That I can't work outside the home?"

"I'm just saying that this isn't right."

"You're doing what you want, and so can I."

That night, I dreamt about my mother. When I awoke, I couldn't remember the details of the dream except that I had wanted to phone her. I had picked up the phone, but I hadn't known the number. So, I held the phone in my hand, stupidly, unwilling to return it to the cradle.

The next day was Saturday, our busiest day in the shop. Ellen was pleasant and worked hard filling orders, packaging groceries, and serving at the counter. Drusilla was a dark, sombre foil to Ellen's good cheer.

That evening, Father and I delivered groceries in the truck.

"So, did you read my letter?" he asked.

"What?"

"My letter to the Synod of Bishops."

"What letter?"

"I gave it to Ellen on Thursday. She didn't give it to you?"

"She never mentioned it."

"Anyway, I laid it on the line about the way they've twisted the Bible and the teachings of Christ. He really had some good points, you know. You should read . . ." Father went on, but if you asked me what he said, I wouldn't be able to tell you. I was doing well to remember when to stop for deliveries, and he had to remind me of a few.

The next day was Sunday. Ellen came downstairs dressed for outdoors. Below her coat I could see the long blue dress that clung to her body and had a fine white lace frill around the throat. "Church?" I asked.

"No, I'm working today."

"Sunday?"

"It's the only day the shop is closed, and artists work on Sunday." She smiled and kissed me on the cheek. "Can I borrow the truck so Phil won't have to pick me up?"

"Sure."

I sat at the kitchen table and watched her drive away. The old-style sash had four panes of glass separated by a cross of wood that held them. The cross looked like a balance scale. In my chest, a balance scale was sinking as more weight was put on the side opposite my heart.

A sudden wisp of white dashed in front of the pane, then another. I stood up and looked in the direction of the departing truck to see the first snow of that year begin to fall in fat wet flakes.

# 15

# Winter

We were studying *Othello*, and I found great comfort in reading the lines of that poor, deceived man. Poetry was another joy, and there I discovered treasures that I wrote about to the great approval of my professors. When marks came out at the Christmas break, I was a contender for the gold medal in English, with the highest marks in the graduate program.

In mid-December, I got a call from Gib Martin. He wanted to see me, so we met in the Spanish Café.

"Man! This brings back memories," I said.

"Memories of mammaries," Gib said as he sized up the girls.

"What did you want?"

"You've been a stranger since you got married. We haven't seen you."

"You know why," I said.

"You hurt Tammy. That's true, but she's got a steady guy now, and even Victoria is coming around."

"What are you studying?" I asked.

"M.A. in economics. I go to Queens for the MBA next September."

"Malacat?"

"MBA program at Queens."

"I saw him in Grand Falls this past August."

Gib put down his Coke. "Now I've got something to tell you," he said. "Billy Crotty's in the mental hospital, and he wants to see you."

"The one on Waterford Bridge Road?"

"Yeah."

"How bad is he?"

"Pretty bad, I guess. I talked to his doctors, and they said he is completely lost in his own world with someone named Alice."

"So, he finally got Alice back," I said.

The next Sunday afternoon, Gib and I went to the Waterford hospital. Snow swirled about our knees as we approached the big brick building.

Outside the front door, a fellow in pyjamas and a parka asked us for a cigarette. Just inside, a gentleman in a straw hat and a light summer suit sat in the lobby with a suitcase at his knee, as if waiting for a flight to Jamaica. A nurse took us under her wing. When we asked to see Billy, she said, "He's very sick, I'm afraid."

"Mentally?" Gib asked.

"Mentally and physically. It's his heart."

She led us to the third floor and unlocked the door to the

ward where Billy Crotty had found his final abode. He was sitting on a bed with his back to us, looking out at the swirling snow.

"You have visitors," the attendant said, and Billy turned around.

"Come over here so I can see you," he said with a frail wave.

As soon as I rounded the bed, he said, "Felix, and look, Gib! Good to see you boys. Good of you to remember your old landlord."

The attendant was pleased. "You're feeling better today, Mr. Crotty."

He ignored her. Gib sat in the only chair, and I sat on the end of Billy's bed. "How are you?" I asked.

"Good and bad. My mind is fooled up, and my ticker is . . . well . . . fooled up too. But it's okay. I don't have to worry about the house, or cooking, or taking my medicine, so that part's good."

"Are they taking good care of you, Mr. Crotty?" Gib asked from the chair.

But Billy spoke to me. "Alice is here."

I said nothing.

"I don't mean really here, physically." He smiled. "I'm not crazy."

"No! You're just here visiting us," I teased him.

He chuckled. "I mean she's in my dreams. Drug-induced, I suppose. Demerol."

"You dream about her?"

"I always have. But now her presence is around me all the time. All around. Like the dancing hearts."

"Hearts?"

"Yes. I'm in a graveyard, and it's nighttime. I see movement and come upon a heart. Big. Almost three feet high, with the two stumps of arteries serving as little legs. He's sad, but he's trying to dance."

"Dance?"

"He hops from leg to leg on those little stumps, and with no music it's pretty hard. But he keeps trying. Crying and trying."

"Do you ever get out of this room?" I asked.

"They take us down to the exercise room twice a week."

"Do you walk, do push-ups, what?"

"My heart is too weak for push-ups. I get tightness in my chest. But I can do a few sit-ups if I use the roller with the head-rest. I take my time. Put my head on the black leather headrest. Know what it's shaped like?"

"No."

"A heart. It's the size of a cow's heart, or a bull's," he said. "Know which one I always take?"

"Which one?"

"The leather is split on one of them. That's the one I pick. It's such a comfort to lay my head back on it. I just rest there for a while before I do a sit-up or two. No one minds. No one else wants it anyway. It's broken."

Then he looked away from me, over Gib's head and out through the barricaded window to the snow devils dancing on the roofs. A smile came over his face, and he said to me, "A comet. This life is just like a comet. You fly in and fly out at great speed. It all happens so fast!" Then he looked back to the window.

Soon, Gib was looking toward the door, and I stood up to

go. Outside Billy's window, secured and wire-meshed, the wind was driving the dry snow in frenzied swirls and whirls around the stone corners.

"Is he crazy or what!" Gib said in the parking lot.

"I guess so," I said.

"Roller bars with broken hearts, and hearts dancing in graveyards! Poor Billy!"

"Yes, poor old Billy," I said, feeling a tightness in my chest.

Early in the New Year, Phil Wallen had his big exhibition in Petley. He held it in his studio, and everyone went, even Mullins the undertaker. No doubt looking for a few inspirational pieces for his funeral home. Ellen went early to help set up the paintings and lay out the hors d'oeuvres, that sort of thing. It was her job, she said.

The paintings were mostly abstracts and made no sense to me. No landscapes, portraits, or people, with one major exception. In the far end of the long, narrow studio, there was a hum of activity and murmuring. I wandered down to see, and a bunch of people moved aside. Before me were four pieces, all dazzling paintings of Ellen.

In the first, she was wearing her blue dress with the lace at the throat and the little buttons. The next one was a large close-up of her head and shoulders. In the last two, she was naked, and that was what the murmuring was about. In one, she was sitting in the lounge chair I could see behind me, and in the other she was reclining on a bed.

I looked around me, and I was alone. I looked back at the paintings of Ellen, whose beauty the artist so faithfully captured. Then I heard a gasp beside me and turned to see Shirley, her hand over her mouth. Father was with her. I said, "Excuse me," and went into the bathroom.

I splashed some water on my face and looked in the mirror. I felt my stomach churn. I vomited into the toilet and flushed quickly, hoping no one had heard. I fixed myself up as best I could and came back into the gallery. Shirley and Father were waiting beside the bathroom door.

"Did you know?" she asked me.

"No."

She took Father's hand. "Walter, I've seen enough art for one day." A lot of people were leaving.

"Philistines," an annoyed Phil Wallen hurled after them.

"Hors d'oeuvre, Felix?" Ellen held the tray.

"Thanks." I took a little wiener on a plastic toothpick.

"Try a little pickle," she said. "They're lovely."

I looked at my pickle, skewered on a toothpick, but could think of nothing else to say or do, so I left without meeting the artist.

Outside, Father and Shirley were waiting in the truck. The windshield and the side mirror had been replaced. Shirley pushed the door open for me. We sat in the cab, as Father pulled out through four inches of dry snow.

Shirley spoke first. "Why don't you come over for a cup of tea, Felix? Ellen will be busy at the exhibit."

"Sure."

The tea was warm and soothing. The wood stove soon had

the kitchen snug, as fresh spruce steamed and whistled in the fire. But Father gulped his tea and said, "Think I'll go out to the stable and get more wood."

Shirley and I had second cups. "You know they're having an affair, don't you," she said.

I just looked at the tea leaves in my cup.

"It's all right if you know and are ready to wait. She may come out of it. All may be well when it's over, if you can get around the pain."

From the stable we could hear the *clomp, clomp, clomp* of Father's axe as he cleaved junks of wood. I knew he was thinking, thinking, thinking about my situation. Thinking for Father was a physical as much as a mental process. He pushed his mind against walls of possibilities and scenarios like a wrestler pushing an opponent in the ring. You could walk into that stable and set it on fire, and he'd still be there cleaving wood when the volunteers arrived in the fire truck.

Shirley and I sipped our tea, silently. *Clomp, clomp, clomp* came from the stable. One thing was certain: Father would eventually come to his conclusion, and when he did, it would make absolutely no sense.

"I love her," I said. "I don't want to lose her."

"Does she love you?"

"I think she likes me. She loves pretending we are Clara and old Wayne White. You know, rich and prosperous pillars of the community."

"My God, Felix, this is not going to work!"

"I know. But she is the most extraordinary thing that has ever happened to me."

*Clomp, clomp, clomp.*

"I wouldn't mind the affair, but the problem is she doesn't care about me. I know she doesn't love me." I started to cry. Jesus, I hate remembering this part. Shirley reached her arm around my neck and pulled my head to her shoulder. I cried in her arms that day, like in the arms of a mother.

Back at the White premises, Ellen was still not home, and I found myself in the flour store. I went upstairs to Dick's workshop and looked at the silent boxes in the corner. I began to take the dolls out and place them, one by one, beside those standing on the floor. It was cold in the unheated building, and I could see my breath in front of me, a grey, silver mist that wafted around my head.

Here was Clara, almost pleasant in her wooden form. Dick had painted a faint smile on her lips. A happy cow popped back into the world, and I placed it on the bare brown floor, not in a grassy meadow. *It's not always the world we want, is it, cow?* I thought.

I found Mullins, Father, Shirley, me, and most strikingly, Ellen. Dick had taken pains to convey not just her physical attributes, but also his love for her. The inner beauty of the doll came not from inside Ellen, but from inside Dick. I placed the figures of me and of Ellen together on the workbench. From there, she and I gazed down on our perfect little village assembled on the floor. But I was shorter than she, because I was only a kid when Dick had created my doll. She looked like a queen on a chessboard, and I a lowly pawn up to her royal waist.

Old Walter White had a big wooden box filled with carpenter's tools, some almost a hundred years old. He used them to create his better world—the world he shared with Clara and Dick. The box also served as a seat, so I sat on it near the window and looked at Dick's wooden Curlew. It was a happy world, replete with more kindness and love than God's attempt.

I took out Dick and placed him on his father's tool box. He stood beside my knee, gazing sadly at the door, as if he were waiting for someone. I thought I had placed him facing his village. A quiet came over me, and I withdrew, like Father, into my own thoughts as I sat on the tool box. It grew dark. A big moon and a million stars peeped in at us, glazing our silent forms with silver. But life's silver breath came from only one of us, the one with the troubled mind.

The window was touched with frost on the bottom corners. The stars shone through the upper glass, reminding me of my mother, and for an instant I felt the warmth of her love like stardust on my face.

"There you are. I looked everywhere for you," Ellen said, staring at me from the door. She ignored Dick's stature at my knee.

"Why?" I asked.

"What are these things?" she asked from the shadows.

"These are dolls Dick made years ago."

"Dick?" She came over and looked at the doll beside me.

"Dick White. Remember him? He's the guy you promised to love for better or worse until death."

"What are you raving about?"

"You promised me the same thing," I said.

"We both made promises." She glared at me.

I had one more thing to say to her. It came hard, but I wanted to say it here, in Dick's workshop, in front of the whole village. "Ellen," I said. "Ellen, it's over."

She pushed the door open without a word, and she was gone. I think she already knew, and it was no great loss to her.

Back in the house, I found her angry. "This didn't have to happen, Felix. If you had gotten your law degree, we would have lived here happy till we died. But you were selfish and went to MUN to be a schoolteacher, like Shirley and your stupid dead mother."

"Well, at least I didn't screw Phil Wallen," I said.

Her eyes narrowed. "I must have been unhappy here with you, or I wouldn't be interested in Phil Wallen. All you were interested in was your precious studies. You ignored me. Phil didn't ignore me."

This was a pointless debate. The deed was already signed. The witnesses were leaving the room. The judge had retired to his chamber.

*Clomp, clomp, clomp* came from the stable as I went into my father's house without knocking.

"Felix, how'd it go?" Shirley asked.

"Okay," I said. "Has he been chopping ever since I left?"

She nodded.

I went out to the stable. Father had his coat hung on a nail and had amassed quite a pile of split wood. Perhaps enough for the rest of the winter. He was splitting the junks of spruce with long, firm swings of a sharp axe. "Father," I shouted, between clomps.

No response. I waited till the axe struck down again, and then I leaped in and took him by the arm. My fingers went around his elbow, and I was surprised how small it was.

His eyes came back to reality. "Felix, boy, how are you? I know. I know. You're depending on me to figure it out, and I will. It's a father's place."

"Then you'll need a lot more wood," I said.

"Humour. Taking it well. That's good. That's good. Be of good cheer." Then he stepped back from me to start swinging again. But I held on to his arm.

"No, it's all right."

"Solved?" he asked.

"Solved!" I said.

"Thank Jesus!" He put down the axe and sagged against the post. "I was just about done in." He didn't even ask me what the solution was. His mind had moved on.

"I might stay here tonight," I said.

"What? Ellen, too?"

"No, just me."

He thought about that for a minute, revisiting the problem before he left it for the last time. "Yes, probably just as well," he said.

Then he took his coat from the nail and put it on. "Come into the house and we'll have a cup of tea." He looked at me, and I thought he was going to put his arm around my shoulder. "Getting too dark to cut wood," he concluded as we stepped into the yard. He shut the stable door behind us and kicked some dry snow against the bottom of the door to keep out the drifts. We walked toward the warm yellow glow from the kitchen window.

Happy as a child, he said, "Wait till we tell Shirley!"

But Shirley already knew that the problem was solved when she heard the last *clomp*.

I was living alone in the old White house when unresolved business brought me to the graveyard one night. I stumbled up the snowy path toward my mother's grave. Low drifts covered the White family, where a large statue of an angel marked their plot as clearly as their shop sign had marked them in life.

Mother's stone was smaller. Black shadows marked her letters chiselled into the white marble and visible even by moonlight.

MARY HELEN RYAN

1923–1954

DEARLY BELOVED WIFE AND MOTHER

I stood up to my knees in snow by her grave and looked at the silent stone.

Then I had a clear memory of when she died. I felt again the strangeness of her absence from our house. A cap left on a chair at morning was there on my return at noon, and there again at suppertime. Nothing moved, with no mother's hand to move it. I remember stopping in the doorway and looking at it like at a ghost.

Father spent most of his time in the stable tending to the horse or chopping wood. I walked into the kitchen one day and looked at the silent dishes and the still-open cupboard door. I said hello to no one, knowing that it was the only word spoken there all day. It was as if life itself had stopped in the house. Like when an elevator stops between floors and you wonder when it will move again and if the little sign will point up or down.

I might have said a prayer for her in the graveyard, but soon I realized that there were no answers there. A rough wind blew ragged clouds across the moon. The stars came out as I found my way back down to the truck.

I drove home but did not go inside the house. I parked the truck on the road and stood for a while looking at the shop. Ellen's arms still splayed across the open door in Phil Wallen's big sign. But icicles now drooped from her feet, and a crust of snow covered her welcoming smile.

I walked around the corner and up past the house to the flour store and the adjoining sheds. One of Clara's Adirondack chairs still sat in a clearing between the drifts. I brushed off the snow and sat down, facing the sheds. Behind me, the road was deserted. I looked at the flour store and thought of the summers that had transpired there with Wayne and Clara, Ellen and me, Ellen and Dick, Ellen and Joe, Dick and his dolls. Something clicked in my head.

I got up and took one more look at the flour store, and I walked down to the old house with a clear purpose. I opened the door with the big key and felt the warmth from the old Maid of Avalon waft around me like memory. The fire had burned down, but there were charred sticks of birch that still flamed and glowed in the bottom of the stove. I took out the two top dampers and the iron centrepiece and slid them to the back of the stove. I put my glove back on, reached in, and pulled out a long birch stick that glowed and flamed red on one end.

In the living room, I touched the glowing rod to the old lace curtains, and they leaped into jubilant flame. Soon the wallpaper caught, and then the dry wainscotting. The varnish from another age bubbled and popped as it burned, and the gases soon drove me from the room. Back in the kitchen, I lit the newspapers behind the stove and dumped kerosene on the floor.

Then I walked out into the January night, the kitchen door left open behind me. From the window, a pink glow was troubling the quiet night. I walked up to the flour store. I passed Clara's Adirondack chair and touched it in a benediction with the fiery rod, and it whispered *tsss* in reply. Inside the flour store, I splashed the old canvas rolls and the four-gallon barrels of tar with kerosene and touched them with my hot birch. I did not go upstairs, but instead came out through the open door and walked down to the shop. The snowy yard was becoming lively as the dancing pink glow replaced black shadows.

I put the key in the brass padlock and let myself into the old shop. I turned on the electric lights, but I did not look around. Instead, I went into the storeroom and sprinkled kerosene on the ancient wood and wallpaper. Then I gave the main store the same treatment, emptying my can on the counter and the brown linoleum. Then I went out into the night with all doors open.

It was about 3:00 a.m., and the house was blazing nicely as the flames romped through the ancient wood and up the back staircase to the second floor. I sat in the Adirondack chair and swung it around so I could see all three conflagrations. Atlanta burned.

It was a good hour before the volunteer fire department arrived with the pumper truck from Petley. They had no siren but ran with the throttle open through the new snow of the yard right up to my chair between the buildings. I turned in my chair, and the first one off the truck, before it even stopped, was Father.

"Felix, boy, are you all right?"

I was about to answer when I saw Fire Chief George Williams unrolling the hose from the pumper. "Let her burn, George," I said, getting up from the chair.

"What, Felix?" he asked without stopping.

"I said let her burn. It's my house, and I can burn it if I want."

"You're foolish, boy!" he said.

The other volunteers were looking at us, but George continued unrolling hose into the snow.

I went over to him and put my hand on his shoulder. "George, I set the fire myself, and I want it to burn down."

"Jesus Christ, Felix!" He was spitting in confused excitement.

Then Father stood by my side. "George, he wants to burn it down. There are no houses or trees nearby, there's no wind. I'd say he picked a good night for it."

Father's logic always defied logic.

George turned away from him and said to me, "Is there anybody in any of those buildings?"

"No," I said.

"In the house?"

"Nobody. Just ghosts."

"Damn it! This'll cost me my job." He threw the nozzle into the snow.

"What job? You're a volunteer, George, like the rest of us," someone said. Others laughed.

So, I sat in the chair, and the firemen sat on top of the pumper or in the cab and watched the show. Once, they had to move the truck when the roof caught and pieces of burning felt flew into the yard. I looked behind me and saw Father still standing by my chair.

The fire reached the second floor of the flour store. Flames licked out through the windows and soon from the window of Dick's carpentry shop. The warm air stroked my face, and I may have dozed off in the chair. As the pink turned to orange, I looked to the window and thought I saw a face or a doll. I looked closely, but then the window burst with the heat, and glass blew out across the snow. I thought I saw Dick's face through the smoke. Between baffles I saw it look toward me, and the strangest thing—his sad face had changed into a smile. Then all was covered by the thick smoke as the roof caught and the tar and felt began to boil and burn.

The sheds were soon burning, and the brightest part of the night was the hour or two when all the roofs burned together in one great alleluia of sound and light. Perhaps visible from outer space—my sign to the stars. I finally had a sign on my own house.

I dozed off for a while, and the winter dawn found us still there. The place was levelled to the sooty snow. The volunteers kicked and poked through the charred remains of what looked like three huge cremation sites. Then the men went home to breakfast.

Father was walking about. "Want some breakfast, Felix?" he asked. I got out of the chair, stiff and weary. We went down to his truck, and he started the engine.

"What do you think?" I asked him.

"Yes, good idea! It's often a good idea to start afresh! Something biblical about it. I must remember to look it up." His mind was already travelling in a new orbit around the sun.

In 2000, *The Plains of Madness*, a work of historical fiction, won the inaugural Percy Janes Award for best novel manuscript in Newfoundland. His short story *The Sign on My Father's House* was published as a winning entry in *Canadian Storyteller*, Toronto, in the summer of 2004.

Other books include *The Black Heart*, a collection of poetry, and *Wilfred Grenfell*, a children's biography, published by Fitzhenry & Whiteside.

His poems have been used as operatic song settings nationally and internationally: poems *Ancestors*, *Songs*, and *Caplin Scull* were broadcast on CBC radio by Lyn Channing of the Music Department, University of Calgary; and his poem *Songs* was presented by Peter Mannion and the Galway University Choir in Ireland. *Ancestors* was read at the welcoming ceremony for Her Majesty Queen Elizabeth II when she visited Newfoundland and Labrador.

Tom Moore was born in St. John's, Newfoundland, in 1950. His first novel, *Good-bye Momma*, became a Canadian bestseller. It was chosen as a "Children's Choice" by the Children's Book Centre in Toronto and was translated into Danish by Munksgaard Publishers of Copenhagen in 1982. It was later translated into Romanian by Cite Libra Publishers. The CBC produced a radio play version broadcast nationally. The Canadian Book of Lists called it one of the ten best children's books in Canada.

In 1994, *Angels Crying* became Moore's second national bestseller. It is the true story of his student, a sexual assault victim. It has become a case study for a number of university schools of social work, including Memorial University, Dalhousie University, College of the North Atlantic, and the University of Maine at Presque Isle. It was translated into Chinese by New Sprouts Publishers of Taipei in 2002. (*continued*)